Praise for Debbie Macomber and

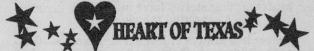
HEART OF TEXAS

"Reading a book by Debbie Macomber reminds me of watching those wonderful Tracy-Hepburn movies with strong lovable characters, quick-paced dialogue and the hard-won happily-ever-after. With Shirley, Goodness and Mercy, Debbie gave us a delightful glimpse of heaven; I can hardly wait to see what she does for Texas."
—Mary Lynn Baxter

"Romance readers everywhere cherish the books of Debbie Macomber."
—Susan Elizabeth Phillips

"Debbie Macomber writes stories as grand as Texas itself."
—Pamela Morsi

"Debbie Macomber writes characters who are as warm and funny as your best friends. She's earned her place as one of today's most beloved authors."
—Susan Wiggs

"Every Debbie Macomber novel is a *don't miss* read."
—Katherine Stone

"Debbie Macomber is one of the few true originals in women's fiction. Her books are filled with warmth and tenderness, full of sweet characterizations that melt the heart and never cloy. Her books are touching and marvelous and not to be missed."
—Anne Stuart

"Debbie Macomber's name on a book is a guarantee of delightful, warmhearted romance."
—Jayne Ann Krentz

"I've never met a Macomber book I didn't love!"
—Linda Lael Miller

Debbie Macomber is one of America's most popular authors. In fact, her appealing characters and heartwarming stories have made her a favorite around the globe.

Debbie has always enjoyed telling stories—first to the children she baby-sat as a young teen and later to her own kids. As a full-time wife and mother and avid romance reader, she dreamed of one day sharing her stories with a wider audience. She sold her first book in 1982—and that was only the beginning!

Today there are more than 40 million copies of her books in print.

Debbie loves to hear from her readers. You can reach her at P.O. Box 1458, Port Orchard, Washington 98366

HEART OF TEXAS

Books in order of publication:

Lonesome Cowboy
Texas Two-Step
Caroline's Child
Dr. Texas
Nell's Cowboy
Lone Star Baby

11-14-21
S
8/00

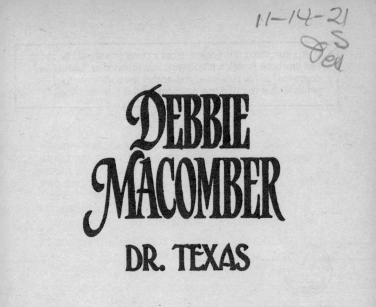

DEBBIE MACOMBER

DR. TEXAS

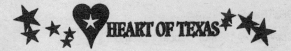

HEART OF TEXAS

Harlequin Books

TORONTO • NEW YORK • LONDON
AMSTERDAM • PARIS • SYDNEY • HAMBURG
STOCKHOLM • ATHENS • TOKYO • MILAN
MADRID • WARSAW • BUDAPEST • AUCKLAND

ISBN 0-373-83345-8

DR. TEXAS

Printed in U.S.A.

Dearest Friends,

After the success of MIDNIGHT SONS, and those stubborn Alaskan men, Harlequin approached me about doing another six-book series. But where was I going to find heroes to match those strong, endearing bush pilots? The answer wasn't long in coming. I've always had a weakness for cowboys, and no place on earth grows 'em quite like Texas.

So, my friends, here they are: the men and women of Promise, Texas. Situated deep in the Texas hill country, Promise is truly a town with heart, populated by people like you and me— hardworking, proud and just a little sassy. A town with an interesting past and an exciting future.

For the MIDNIGHT SONS series, my husband and I traveled to Alaska. This time around, I conned my editor, Paula Eykelhof, into exploring Texas with me. With a rental car, a map and the sense of direction of a pet rock, Paula and I toured the Texas hill country. We met the people, sampled the barbecues, tasted the wines and gazed endlessly at cowboys. If this wasn't heaven, then we were pretty darn close!

So I invite you to sit back, put your feet up and allow me to introduce you to a few of those Texan cowboys. The men of Alaska started this craziness, but the men in Texas refuse to be outdone. They're just as stubborn, just as ornery, just as proud. And just as lovable.

Enjoy.

Debbie Macomber

THE PEOPLE OF PROMISE: CAST OF CHARACTERS

Nell Bishop: thirty-something widow with a son, Jeremy, and a daughter, Emma. Her husband died in a tractor accident.

Ruth Bishop: Nell's mother-in-law. Lives with Nell and her two children.

Dovie Boyd: runs an antiques shop and has dated Sheriff Frank Hennessy for ten years

Caroline Daniels: postmistress of Promise

Maggie Daniels: Caroline's five-year-old daughter

Dr. Jane Dickinson: new doctor in Promise

Ellie Frasier: owner of Frasier's Feed Store

Frank Hennessy: local sheriff

Max Jordan: owner of Jordan's Towne & Country

Wade McMillen: preacher of Promise Christian Church

Edwina and Lily Moorhouse: sisters. Retired schoolteachers.

Cal and Glen Patterson: local ranchers. Brothers who ranch together.

Phil and Mary Patterson: parents of Cal and Glen. Operate a local B&B.

Louise Powell: town gossip

Wiley Rogers: sixty-year-old ranch foreman at the Weston ranch

Laredo Smith: wrangler hired by Savannah Weston

Barbara and Melvin Weston: mother and father to Savannah, Grady and Richard. The Westons died six years ago.

Richard Weston: youngest of the Weston siblings

Savannah Weston: Grady and Richard's sister. Cultivates old roses.

Grady Weston: rancher and oldest of the Weston siblings

Chapter One

Texas is the only state big enough to hold your dreams. Someone had told Dr. Jane Dickinson that when she signed up for this gig. But whoever it was obviously hadn't lived in Promise.

With medical-school bills the size of the national debt, signing a three-year agreement to practice medicine in the Texas hill country in exchange for partial payment had seemed the perfect solution. Whatever romanticizing she'd done when she'd first thought about making the move from urban California to the heart of rural America had faded with the reality of her situation. Texas had bugs practically as big as pit bulls and she'd always been somewhat phobic about insects, whether they were of the crawling or flying variety. More serious, more disturbing, was the fact that she simply didn't fit in with this community. People were never less than polite, but they hadn't accepted her. They came to her as a last resort—if they couldn't cure whatever ailed them on their own—and then complained because she wasn't Doc Cummings. Being fresh out of medical school, female and a good fifty years younger than the beloved practitioner hadn't helped, either.

But although Jane was lonely and often at loose ends, she felt that she'd begun to make strides. Becoming friends with Dovie Boyd had a lot to do with that. The older woman owned an antique shop with the small Victorian Tea Room tucked in one corner, and she'd generously offered Jane not only friendship but advice. Life had taken a decided turn for the better since that first morning Jane had spoken to Dovie.

Her last scheduled patient for the day had left, and so had Jenny Bender, her receptionist. Jane sat at her desk, leaning comfortably back in her chair. The makeup she'd applied that morning had long since dissolved in sweat, and her feet ached. It'd been a busy day, which was a good sign. It meant that more people of Promise were coming to trust her skills.

Ellie Patterson was due to return from her honeymoon this week, too. Her second new friend was a local businesswoman. They'd recently met, thanks to Dovie. Jane liked Ellie's no-nonsense approach to life, her quick wit and down-to-earth attitude. After having lunch together, Jane could tell they had the potential to become good friends. She hoped that was the case, because at this point, she needed all the friends she could get.

A distinct noise in the outer office cut into her thoughts, and Jane stood up to investigate.

"Is someone here?" she called, walking out of her office.

Nothing.

"Hello," she tried again, wondering if she was beginning to hear things.

"Dr. Jane?" A child's voice came from the waiting room.

Jane found six-year-old Maggie Daniels standing just inside the clinic door. "Oh, hi, Maggie."

The little girl's pigtails fell forward as she lowered her head. "Hello."

Maggie's mother was Promise's postmistress, and the post office was next door to the health clinic. She'd talked to Caroline Daniels a number of times, and had heard just a day or two ago that Caroline and a local cattle rancher, Grady Weston, were now engaged.

"Where's your mother?" Jane asked. It was unusual for Maggie to come to the clinic by herself.

"At work," she answered, still keeping her head lowered. Her arms were wrapped protectively around her stomach.

Jane knelt down in front of her. "Are you feeling all right, Maggie?"

The little girl shook her head.

"Where do you feel sick?"

"My tummy."

Jane brushed the hair from the child's forehead and checked for fever. Maggie's skin was cool to the touch. "Does your mommy know you're here?"

Maggie's head flew up, her eyes wide with alarm. "No! Please don't tell her, okay?"

"But if she doesn't know where you are, she might worry."

"She said I could play while she finished work.

Mrs. Murphy had to drop me off early today 'cause she had a dentist appointment."

Jane assumed Mrs. Murphy baby-sat Maggie after school.

"Is something at school bothering you?" Jane guessed, thinking this stomachache might be linked to an incident there. School had been in session a little more than two weeks. That Maggie didn't want her mother to know where she was aroused Jane's suspicions. Perhaps Maggie had gotten into trouble with her teacher and was worried about what would happen when her mother found out. Either that, or she suffered doubts or fears regarding her mother's recent engagement.

"I like school," Maggie said, and her face brightened. "I'm in first grade this year."

"But you're not feeling well?"

The little girl shook her head, sending her pigtails swaying. "My tummy hurts."

"Okay," Jane said. "Maybe we'd better have a look." She held out her hand to Maggie, who slipped her own small one into Jane's.

"You won't tell Mommy?" Maggie pleaded again.

"Not if you don't want me to," Jane said, although she wondered if it was wise to make such a promise. But it was clear the child was deeply upset about something. While Jane didn't have a lot of training in pediatrics, she suspected that if she hadn't reassured Maggie, the child would have bolted.

Playing the situation by ear, Jane led Maggie into

the examination room and lifted her easily onto the table.

"Take off your backpack and I'll listen to your tummy," Jane instructed, picking up her stethoscope.

Slowly and with obvious reluctance Maggie did as she was asked, but when Jane went to move the backpack off the table, Maggie grabbed it back and clung to it. Jane realized immediately that whatever bothered the child was in that backpack.

"Is there something important in your bag?" Jane asked casually.

Maggie nodded. She tucked her chin tight against her chest. Finally, hesitantly, Maggie opened the zipper. Twice she paused and glanced up at Jane as if questioning the wisdom of continuing.

Jane allowed the girl to make the decision on her own. Apparently Maggie had decided to trust her, because once she had the bag completely open, she withdrew an old dilapidated-looking doll. It was either a replica of an antique or the genuine thing, although that didn't seem likely. Either way, the doll had seen better days. It was falling apart. The face appeared hand-stitched, the once red lips faded to a pale pink. The muslin dress had probably been white but was now a washed-out shade of yellow. The dull calico apron had frayed edges. Despite its condition, the doll had a certain appeal. At one time it must have been the much-loved toy of some young girl.

"I want you to keep it," Maggie said in a small tense voice as she held out the doll.

"But I couldn't do that," Jane protested.

"Please..." Big tears welled in Maggie's dark

eyes. "I took it..." She clutched her stomach with both arms. "I'm sorry for taking her away from—" She stopped and her lower lip started to wobble, but she quickly pulled her emotions together.

"Can't you take it back to the person it belongs to?" Jane asked.

Maggie shook her head vigorously, the pigtails whipping about her face.

Jane frowned. "So you want me to keep her for you?"

Maggie nodded.

Perhaps that was the best solution. Again Jane followed her instincts, which told her that pressing Maggie to tell her anything more was a mistake. The little girl clearly regretted having taken the doll and wasn't sure how to handle the situation now.

"All right. I'll do that." She could display the old doll in her office in the hope that whoever owned it would come to her and ask. That would save Maggie the embarrassment of having to return it.

"I promise to take good care of your friend," Jane said solemnly. She helped Maggie down from the table. "Come on, let's find a new home for your doll." Perhaps later Jane could make a few discreet inquiries. Dovie might know something or have a suggestion, since she owned an antique shop—although the older woman seemed unusually distracted at the moment. Jane assumed it had something to do with Frank Hennessey, the local sheriff, who'd been Dovie's longtime male friend. Apparently they'd had some kind of argument and were no longer seeing each other.

Maggie slipped her hand into Jane's as they walked into the small office once occupied by Doc Cummings. The most logical place to set the doll was on the bookshelf, which looked out into the hallway. Anyone passing by was sure to see it.

Carefully Jane put the toy on the top shelf. "Okay," she said, and took a step back. "What do you think?"

The youngster smiled and released a great sigh. "My tummy doesn't hurt anymore."

"That's wonderful." A miracle cure, Jane mused; she must be a better doctor than she'd imagined. "If you want to come and visit your friend, you're welcome to do that any time," Jane told her.

Maggie shook her head, then whirled around. "Mommy's calling," she said. Racing down the hallway, she grabbed her backpack from the examination table and flew toward the waiting room. She paused abruptly and looked back. "Thank you, Dr. Jane."

"You're welcome," Jane said with a smile.

Then Maggie disappeared out the door.

If only dealing with her other patients was this easy.

DOVIE BOYD was miserable. She wandered between the lush rows of her garden, picking ripe tomatoes from her heavily laden plants. Her only consolation was that Frank Hennessey probably felt even worse than she did. For ten years they'd been friends. More than friends. During those years they'd talked frequently of marriage—with Dovie generally bringing up the subject. Frank had been a bachelor all his life; Dovie understood that marriage would be a big change for him and had been patient. No, she thought now, she'd been stupid. Although she loved Frank, she'd never been completely comfortable with their arrangement. He knew that, which must be why he'd made promises he didn't intend to keep. When she pressured him about it after Ellie Frasier and Glen Patterson's wedding, he owned up to the fact that he simply couldn't marry her. He loved her, he claimed, but he wasn't the marrying kind. He just couldn't do it.

The truth had been painful, but she'd lived long enough to recognize something else. Either she accepted Frank and their relationship the way it was or she broke it off.

She broke it off. Not that it was an easy decision. She missed him. Missed their afternoon chats over coffee, missed their romantic dinners and sitting on the porch gazing at the stars, sipping a nice glass of East Texas wine. She missed cuddling up with him at night, too. For the better part of nine years Frank had spent two nights a week with her.

Her twenty-six year marriage to Marvin had been a good one, although to her regret they'd remained childless. She'd loved her husband and grieved deeply for him when he died.

That was thirteen years ago. She'd still been young enough then to want a man in her life—was young enough still! Frank had courted her for two years before they'd become lovers. She would never have believed she'd allow a man into her bed without the benefit of a wedding band. But she had, trusting with all her heart that Frank would one day marry her. In retrospect she wondered how she could have let the arrangement continue this long.

In other years Dovie would pick two or three large green tomatoes for Frank; this year she left them to ripen on the vine. There wouldn't be any fried green tomatoes for Frank Hennessey. The thought saddened her, reminding her that there was a gap in her life, that she'd lost an important person. But this break, no matter how painful, was necessary, she told herself.

Just then Frank's patrol car rounded the corner and Dovie's heart accelerated. Although tempted, she looked away, pretending not to notice.

"Hello, Dovie," he called softly.

She glanced in his direction. He'd come to a stop and rolled down the car window.

"How are you?" he asked in that sweet seductive way he had. He'd always used that tone when he wanted Dovie to know how much he loved her.

Slowly she turned to look at him. "Very well. Thank you for asking," she said, then continued down the row, picking tomatoes. No sooner had the words left her lips when she heard his car door slam. It demanded an effort of will not to get up and move toward him. She fought a desperate urge to stare at him, to indulge her heart and her eyes. Frank was a fine-looking man even now as he neared retirement age. He'd maintained a trim physique and most people wouldn't guess he was sixty.

"Seems your garden has a lot of tomatoes this year," he commented. He remained on the sidewalk, following her from the opposite side of the picket fence.

"Seems that way," she said after a moment, wondering at the wisdom of allowing this conversation. All it did was remind her how unhappy she was without Frank, how much she missed him. From the glances he sent her, she knew he missed her, too. She also knew he was trying to wear down her resolve.

"How've you been?" Frank pressed when she didn't elaborate on the abundance of her garden.

"Wonderful." She prayed God would forgive her the lie.

"I'm afraid I can't say the same. I miss you, Dovie. Nothing seems right without you."

Nothing seemed right for her, either, but she wasn't about to admit it. What made this breakup so difficult was that she loved Frank. Despite that, she couldn't go on with their arrangement. It wasn't the life she wanted. She craved what most women of her generation did—and maybe most women, period. Commitment, emotional security, an open acknowledgement of love.

"I miss you, sweetheart," he said again, in a soft sad voice.

"Then marry me, Frank."

His eyes narrowed. "We've been through this a hundred times. Dovie, you know how I feel about you. I'd give my life for you. You're the best thing that's ever happened to me. If I were to marry anyone, it'd be you, but I *can't* Dovie, I just can't."

It hurt to hear the words, but she was glad he'd said them because this forced her to remember that nothing would ever change between them.

"I love you, Dovie! I'm doing my damnedest to

understand why everything's different and all because I told you the truth. None of this would've happened if I hadn't admitted I couldn't go through with marriage."

"We've already said everything that needs to be said," she told him, shifting the weight of the basket from one arm to the other.

"Let me help you with that," Frank offered. "That's much too heavy for you."

He was halfway to the gate before she stopped him. "I can manage on my own."

He gripped two pickets so tightly that his knuckles whitened. His blue eyes implored her. "Dovie, please."

Already she could feel herself weakening, and she forced herself to be strong. It'd been less than two weeks. Sooner or later Frank would understand. This wasn't a game, or an ultimatum or an attempt to manipulate him. They just saw things differently; it was as simple as that. He'd made his decision and she'd made hers. He would simply have to accept that she wasn't giving in or changing her mind.

"I need to go inside. Good seeing you again, Frank. I hope you have a pleasant evening." Then she headed toward the house and didn't look back.

After setting the tomatoes by the sink, Dovie reached for her phone and punched in her bestfriend's number.

Mary Patterson operated the local bed-and-breakfast with her husband, Phil, and the couple had been friends of Dovie's for years. Although Dovie was well aware that others knew of her arrangement with

Frank, the only person she'd actually confided in was Mary.

"Frank was just here," Dovie announced when Mary answered the phone. Her hand clenched the receiver and she closed her eyes, distressed by the brief confrontation. It had left her feeling weak and light-headed.

"What did he say?" Mary asked.

"That he misses me and wishes things could go back the way they were before."

"You refused to listen, right?"

"Right," Dovie answered.

"Good!" Mary said with conviction. "That's exactly what you *should* do."

Her support was something Dovie badly needed just then. "He said he's miserable."

"As well he ought to be!"

"I am, too, but I suppose I'm more determined than I am miserable."

"Oh, Dovie." Mary's voice was full of sympathy. "I know how hard this is on you. But Frank's strung you along all these years, promising to marry you, and then he decides he can't go through with it. You should sue him for breach of promise."

"I wouldn't do that."

"I know."

"It's just that I feel so alone," Dovie confessed. "In some ways this is as difficult as when Marvin died."

"This *is* a death," Mary said compassionately. "The death of a relationship."

Her friend was right, Dovie realized sadly. She'd been able to bury her husband, lay him and their lives together to rest. She'd taken the time she needed to heal, the time she'd needed to grieve, and then, when the worst of the pain was over, she'd opened her antique shop. Starting the business had helped her get through the first lonely year. What she needed now, Dovie decided, was a diversion, something that would see her through the long difficult weeks ahead.

"I'm thinking of traveling," Dovie announced, although the thought had only just come to her.

"Traveling?" Mary echoed. "Where?"

"I'm not sure—possibly Europe. I've heard about the wonderful antiques you can get there. I'll make it a buying trip," she said, warming to the idea. Not only would it be her first trip abroad, she'd be able to write it off as a tax deduction.

"When?" Mary asked.

"I...I'm not sure yet, but I'll talk to Gayla Perkins at Adventure Travel in the morning."

"Dovie..." For the first time Mary hesitated. "This sounds drastic."

"I need to do *something* different," Dovie said. "Otherwise I'm afraid I'll give in to Frank."

"Will you travel alone?" Mary asked.

Dovie hadn't gotten that far in her planning. "It looks like I'll have to."

"Take a cruise, then," Mary advised.

"A cruise?" Dovie hadn't thought of that. "I don't know..."

"You might meet someone." Mary's voice rose with enthusiasm. "They have short ones, three and four days. I understand the prices are reasonable and there's plenty of single men."

Dovie didn't want any other man in her life.

"A cruise would be perfect for you," Mary went on. "I read not long ago about certain cruises that specialize in matching up singles. That'd be ideal."

"Oh, Mary, I don't know..."

"What's not to know? You want to travel, and if that's the case, then do it in style."

"A cruise," Dovie said slowly, letting the idea grow more familiar.

"Not just an ordinary cruise," Mary corrected, "but a short one especially for singles. Can you imagine how Frank's going to feel when he hears about that?"

Dovie figured she had no business caring about Frank's feelings one way or the other, but she did. A dozen times a day she had to remind herself that Frank Hennessey was no longer part of her life. They were no longer a couple. She had her own life to live, and the time had come for her to explore other possibilities. Yes, a singles cruise could be just the thing.

"I'll do it," Dovie said. "First thing tomorrow. I'll call Adventure Travel."

"You won't be sorry," her friend assured her.

Dovie had a strong feeling Mary was right.

THE ALARM WOKE Cal Patterson at the usual hour. He rolled out of bed and stretched his arms high above his head, yawning loudly. On his way into the bathroom, he caught his reflection in the mirror and stopped to stare at himself. Hmm. Not much to look at. He wondered at this sudden need to examine his features. Probably had to do with Glen and Ellie getting married, he decided.

He'd grown pensive since the wedding. He'd found himself entertaining a number of intriguing notions after Ellie and his brother had left on their honeymoon. Like the fact that he missed Glen. Really missed him.

Glen. Married.

Even after the wedding, it still didn't seem possible. They were brothers and partners in the Lonesome Coyote Ranch. Both had been born here, and as far as Cal was concerned he'd die here, too. The ranch was his life, his blood, his soul.

Glen was like him, a rancher at heart. Their ancestors had settled in Texas a century and a half before, and the family had been ranching one spread or another ever since. When the time was right, Cal suspected Glen would buy his own ranch, one closer to town since Ellie would need to travel in every day.

Cal had finished dressing when he heard a door close downstairs.

"Don't tell me you're still sleeping?" a voice called up. "What the hell kind of ranch are you running here?"

Glen? His brother was supposed to be on his honeymoon! Cal started down the stairs. "What are you doing here?" Cal shouted.

"I go away for a few days and this whole place goes to hell in a handbasket."

Cal reached the bottom of the stairs, and the two brothers stared at each other. It'd barely been ten days since the wedding and yet it felt as if they'd been apart for ten years. They hugged with the fierce love of brothers who were also close friends.

"How was the Gulf?" Cal asked, breaking away and moving toward the kitchen to make a pot of coffee.

"Terrific," Glen said, "although Ellie and I didn't get outside much."

Cal hadn't expected that they would, seeing as this was their honeymoon. "I didn't think you were due back for a couple of days yet."

"We weren't, but you know Ellie. She was worried about the feed store."

"And you were worried about the ranch."

Glen rubbed the side of his jaw. "Not...worried, exactly."

The two laughed and Cal grabbed a couple of mugs. "So, is married life everything you hoped for?"

"More," Glen said wistfully. "I knew I loved Ellie," he continued, his voice thoughtful, "but I didn't realize exactly how much until this past week. I feel like I'm the luckiest man alive. Hey, Cal? You might want to think about making the leap one day yourself."

Cal let the comment slide and poured them each a cup of coffee. He handed one to his brother. "Ellie is special," he said.

Glen sugared his coffee, and they talked business for the next forty minutes, then headed to the barn for the start of their day.

By the afternoon it was difficult for Cal to remember that Glen had ever been away. They'd worked together for so many years they didn't require words to communicate. As soon as they'd finished delousing the calves, Glen made a beeline for the barn and his favorite gelding, Moonshine. He groomed the big bay, then washed up. "I'll see you in the morning," he said on his way out of the barn.

Cal grinned to himself at his brother's eagerness to hurry home to his bride. "Sure thing," he said, waving him off. Although Glen had spent most of his free time with Ellie before they got married, she'd often driven out to the ranch. Cal had enjoyed watching their exchanges, and he'd especially relished being the beneficiary of Ellie's delicious homemade dinners. She'd taken a few cooking lessons from Dovie, mostly in preparing basic meals, the kind Cal liked. Well, she could practice on him as often as she wanted. He wasn't much of a cook himself, but managed to fry up a decent steak every so often.

"Damn, I almost forgot," Glen said halfway out the barn door. "Ellie wanted me to ask if you had plans Friday night."

"Plans?"

"For dinner," Glen answered, as if that should be obvious.

"I don't have anything special going," he said. Already his mind was full of the meals she'd served in the weeks leading up to the wedding. Memories of her roast chicken and garlic mashed potatoes made his mouth water. "If she's thinking of inviting me over, you tell her I accept."

Glen looked surprised. "You sure about this?"

"Why shouldn't I be?"

"Well..." Glen's mouth widened in a grin and

he slowly shook his head. "No reason. I'll tell Ellie to count on you for Friday night."

"You do that."

Cal walked his brother out. He stood there for a moment, watching the dust plume as Glen's truck barreled out of the yard and down the long driveway. Not for the first time in the past ten days Cal wondered what his own life would be like now if he'd married Jennifer Healy.

Two years earlier Cal had been engaged. But less than forty-eight hours before the wedding Jennifer had changed her mind and abruptly left town. She'd given him no explanation.

But Cal knew why she'd done it. She'd wanted him to be something he never could.

He'd loved her, or had convinced himself he did. But she'd had other plans for him, plans she didn't divulge until the wedding arrangements were made. Jennifer seemed to believe that once they were husband and wife, she'd be able to convince him to sell his half of the ranch to Glen. Her scheme included moving him to San Antonio or Houston. Even now, two years later, Cal couldn't imagine himself living in big-city America. It shocked him that a woman he loved, the woman he'd intended to marry, didn't understand that a city the size of Houston would slowly kill him. He was a country boy, through and through.

When he'd adamantly refused to give in to her demands, Jennifer had walked out, leaving him to deal with the embarrassment of canceling the wedding at the last minute. And yet—perhaps it was ego, he didn't know—he had the distinct feeling that if he'd asked, she might have stayed.

But he hadn't asked, hadn't believed the relationship was worth saving. Her preference for leaving the ranch, leaving Promise, would have always been an issue between them. She would have held his decision against him and they'd have argued about it again and again. So he'd let her go. He realized in that moment that he'd given his heart to a woman who would have abused his love.

After Jennifer left, his attitude toward women had undergone a swift change. He found them untrustworthy and deceptive. Glen and others had tried to convince him that not all woman were like Jennifer. Deep down Cal believed that, but he wasn't willing to give anyone that kind of power over him a second time. He'd learned his lesson well.

His new sister-in-law was an exception. He'd always been fond of Ellie and was understandably proud that he was the one to figure out how Glen and Ellie felt about each other long before either of them had a clue. Actually, considering how anti-romance he'd become, that was little short of amazing.

Ellie was a sweetheart and Glen was a lucky man. His sister-in-law was an idealist, though. She firmly believed in the power of love. While that might prove true for others, it hadn't for him.

Cal never intended to marry. He was thirty-six and set in his ways. His life was full and he didn't have room in it for a relationship; he'd made damn sure of that. Whenever he was tempted to let his guard down and fraternize with the enemy, something would happen to remind him that women weren't to be trusted.

Given time, he thought cynically, ninety-nine percent of the female population would turn on a man. He'd seen it happen. Well, maybe not in Promise— not often, anyway. He could actually think of a few success stories. Glen, of course. His parents. Savannah Weston and Laredo Smith. And now his best friend, Grady Weston, was engaged to Caroline Daniels; he supposed their marriage stood a chance if anyone's did. But he was still convinced he was right. Anyway, Texas men weren't prone to "sharing their pain." You wouldn't find a cowboy crying his eyes out on some talk show about a woman who'd done him wrong. In Texas men sat around and drowned their sorrows in beer. If they mentioned their troubles, it was in words no television channel could air. And ten to one, if a man had problems, there was a woman involved.

Cal headed back to the house. He'd grab something easy for dinner and then tackle some paperwork. Come Friday, Ellie would be cooking up something memorable.

He paused in his tracks as he recalled that sly smile of Glen's when he'd asked about Ellie's cooking.

Then it hit him like the proverbial bolt of lightning. Ellie had invited him all right, but no one had said anything about her doing any cooking. His brand-new sister-in-law intended to set him up with one of her girlfriends. She was fixing to play matchmaker.

It'd be a cold day in hell before Cal would sit still for that.

Chapter Two

Jane was astounded—and delighted. Only two days home from her honeymoon, and Ellie Frasier Patterson had already dropped in to visit her. Jane was between patient appointments, so she and Ellie spent a few minutes catching up on news. Then Ellie announced that Jane would be joining her and Glen for dinner that Friday night.

"But—"

"You don't have an option here," Ellie said with a grin. "You need a Texas education and you're going to get it."

Jane took half a second to think it over. "I'll be there." She'd asked for help. Why turn it down when it was offered?

"Be at the Chili Pepper at seven Friday night," Ellie instructed on her way out the door.

Jane made a note in her weekly planner, then sat back in her chair with a triumphant smile. Finally, after spending six months in this town, she was making progress. This would be her first night out with people her own age, and she looked forward to it.

On Friday night she arrived at the restaurant pre-

cisely at seven. The place was packed. She glanced
around and then saw Ellie wave her arm to get her
attention. Ellie, her husband, Glen, and a man Jane
recognized as Glen's brother were sitting in a booth
in a far corner. Jane waved back and wove her way
between the tables toward them.

"Hello," she said, raising her voice to be heard
above the country-and-western tunes blaring from
the jukebox.

"You remember Glen," Ellie said, indicating the
man sitting next to her. "And my brother-in-law,
Cal."

"It's good to see you both again," Jane said,
smiling brightly.

The rancher stood—reluctantly, Jane thought—to
allow her to slide into the booth next to the wall,
opposite Ellie. It concerned her a little that Ellie
hadn't said anything about this being a double date;
Jane wondered if Ellie's brother-in-law had been
kept equally in the dark. Probably, or he wouldn't
be here. She'd seen him around before, and although
she hadn't known his name until now, she thought
Cal Patterson was one of the rudest unfriendliest
men she'd ever *not* met.

He was good-looking, or could be if he bothered
to smile. Tall and lean, he had that rough-and-
tumble cowboy appeal.

One glance from Cal gave her the answer she'd
suspected. He, too, had been duped, but judging by
his fierce scowl, he thought she was in cahoots with
Ellie.

Jane's high hopes for the evening died a sudden
and painful death.

"I'm so glad you could make it," Ellie said, and handed Jane a menu. Cal sat next to her as stiff as new rope and about as welcoming.

The waitress brought over a pitcher of beer and four mugs. Willie Nelson's plaintive voice rolled from the jukebox just then, and Jane's mouth gaped in astonishment as the entire restaurant began to sing along with him. She would've joined them had she known the words.

"If you're going to live in Texas you gotta love Willie Nelson," Ellie informed her when the tune was finished.

"Not just Willie, either," Glen added, "but country music in general."

"I like Garth Brooks," Jane told them, although she was familiar with only a couple of his songs. "And Johnny Cash."

"That's a good start," Glen said, giving her a friendly smile. He lifted a mug to his lips, having waited for the froth to settle, and Jane reached for her own. She wasn't much of a beer drinker, preferring white wine, but when in Rome…

Cal sampled his beer, too. "If you're serious about living in Texas, then you'll need at least one button on your car radio set to a country-and-western station."

Jane was surprised by his remark. "I am serious," she told him. Other than an awkward greeting, this was the first time he'd spoken directly to her.

"She wasn't born here," Ellie said, smiling, "but she came as soon as she could."

Everyone laughed.

The waitress returned for their order—barbecued

ribs, baked beans and coleslaw all around—and soon afterward brought a second pitcher of beer. Jane had yet to finish her first glass, but both men were ready for another.

"What else do I need to do?" Jane asked. "If I want to become a Texan, I mean."

"Clothes are important," Ellie said, "but I can help you with that later."

Jane smoothed her skirt. She'd already learned that lesson the hard way. She'd worn a business suit to a party soon after her arrival and had been sadly overdressed for the occasion. Most everyone else had been in jeans and tank tops. A couple of months later, she'd attended a dance and had dressed casually only to discover it was a formal affair. She'd felt like a fool and stayed no more than a few minutes, feeling completely out of place.

"That's where I've seen you," Cal said. "You were at the party Richard Weston threw for himself, weren't you?"

Jane nodded. She'd only been in town a few days when she'd met a handsome congenial rancher who'd invited her to a party. She hadn't known a soul in Promise, and his was the first friendly face she'd seen. Richard had stopped her on the street and insisted that anyone as beautiful as she was had to come to his party. She'd arrived terribly overdressed and hung around feeling unwelcomed and uncomfortable for more than an hour.

"Whatever happened to Richard?" Jane asked. "I saw him around town a few times, but not recently."

The other three went strangely silent and then exchanged looks as if they weren't sure how much to tell her.

Jane stared at them. "Did I ask something I shouldn't have?" Without knowing it, she'd apparently entered forbidden territory. She couldn't prevent a small sigh from escaping. It'd been this way from the beginning—like being in an alien culture, with no one to guide her or tell her the rules. Or explain the native customs, she thought wryly.

"It's just that Richard Weston is...a sad case."

"Sad?" she echoed dutifully.

"He's all foam and no beer," Glen said. "He's hurt a lot of good people, and worse yet, the ones he's abused most have been his own family."

"Richard arrived back in town after being away six years," Cal muttered. "He made a nuisance of himself and caused a lot of trouble for Grady and Savannah before he disappeared."

"I...I didn't know," Jane said. She'd talked to Richard briefly a couple of times. Their first meeting, when he'd invited her to the party, had been pleasant enough, but the subsequent encounter had left her with the distinct impression that the man was frivolous and irresponsible; apparently her assessment hadn't been far off. She frowned, thinking through the relationships. Okay, Richard was the younger brother of Grady and Savannah, and Savannah was married to...Austin? No, Laredo Smith. Grady had recently become engaged to Caroline Daniels. Even after several months, Jane had a hard time keeping track of all the connections.

"Yeah. Richard disappeared not long ago," Ellie said.

"With Grady's truck," Cal added. "That's Richard for you." He shook his head as though the mere mention of the other man's name disgusted him.

"He stole his own brother's truck?"

"And a lot more." This from Cal, too.

"I don't think we need to worry about him coming back, though," Glen said, sounding sure of himself. "He's gone for good, and all I can say is good riddance."

The others nodded in agreement. A moment of silence followed.

"Do you know about the Bubbas?" Ellie asked, abruptly changing the subject. "Have you met any?"

"Just a couple of the youngsters I've examined who have that nickname."

"There's much more to being a Bubba than a name," Glen told her, grinning once more. "You don't have to be *called* Bubba to be one. There's your basic Bubba, and then there are your different variations, according to what state you live in."

Jane was quickly getting lost. "Perhaps it'd be best if you defined what a Bubba is. A Texas Bubba," she qualified, not wanting to be confused by any other Southern Bubba-types.

"Well," Glen drawled, "that's not as easy as it sounds."

"Sure it is," Cal said. "He drives a beat-up truck with a rifle or fishing pole in the gun rack."

"And carries a fifty-pound sack of dog food in the bed of his truck," Ellie said, "which he probably bought from me."

"He's got a case or two of empty beer and soda

cans rolling around on the floor on the passenger side of the cab.''

"Is he one of those guys who wears a monster belt buckle?" Jane asked eagerly.

Glen and Cal glanced at each other. "All Texans wear giant belt buckles," Glen informed her kindly.

"Yes, I know, but Bubba buckles are smaller and their bellies are bigger."

"You got it!" Ellie and Glen chorused.

Ellie took a swallow of her beer. "So, Jane, you need a bumper sticker. It's not just a Bubba thing. Everyone in Texas has at least one. Three or four are better."

"Okay." This didn't sound difficult. "What should it say?"

"Touch my truck and you die," Cal suggested.

"I don't drive a truck," Jane said with a smile. "I could buy one, though, if I need to."

He grinned, too, and Jane was surprised by the way it transformed his features. Gratified, too. It made him as attractive as she'd guessed it would. "Buying a truck won't be necessary," he told her.

"Insured by Smith and Wesson," Glen said next.

Jane rolled her eyes. "I don't *think* so."

"Don't mess with Texas," Cal continued.

"I think I'd better start taking notes," Jane said in a mock-serious voice, reaching for her purse. This was fun, especially now that Cal seemed to have loosened up some. Was it the beer—or the company?

"She needs a hat," Ellie announced just as their dinner arrived.

"A hat?"

"A lady Stetson," Glen tossed in, and picked up a dripping barbecued rib with both hands.

"A hat doesn't mean a damn thing if she doesn't ride," Cal said as he offered the platter of ribs to Jane.

She helped herself to one, then carefully wiped her fingers on the rather inadequate paper napkin.

"Ride? As in horse?" She looked from Glen to Cal and then to Ellie.

"You're right, Cal," Ellie said, frowning thoughtfully. She nodded in Jane's direction. "You're gonna have to learn to ride."

Jane bit into the pungent smoky-tasting rib, enjoying it more than she would ever have believed. "You're sure about this?" she asked. "I have to ride?"

"Positive."

"Okay," Jane said with some reluctance. "Do you know of anyone who gives lessons?"

"Lessons?" Glen asked, and the three burst into spontaneous laughter.

Jane didn't know what she'd said that was so funny.

"Everyone around here grows up with horses," Ellie explained apologetically. "Most of us were sitting in a saddle before we could walk."

"Then what does someone like me do?"

The question appeared to give them pause. "I don't know," Glen replied at last. "Laredo Smith's raising quarter horses. He might agree to give you lessons."

"I doubt he has the time," Cal inserted. "Laredo and Savannah are building a house, and Laredo's trying to do as much of the work as he can himself. Last I saw they had a good start on it.''

''Well, we need to come up with someone who can teach you to ride,'' Ellie said. She looked sharply at Cal, but Jane noticed that Ellie's brother-in-law was ignoring her. She had a feeling that Ellie'd hoped Cal would jump in and volunteer. Cal didn't, and Jane suspected he wanted nothing more to do with her. It was a pity, because she would have liked to know him better.

CAL HADN'T BEEN KEEN on this evening from the moment he'd realized Ellie wasn't cooking dinner at her own house—and even more so when he figured out she was matching him up with the town doctor. He would've put an end to her less-than-clever method of throwing Dr. Texas in his face if he hadn't worried about annoying his new sister-in-law. He'd known Ellie for years, but the relationship was different now, and he had to respect that. When the evening was over, he'd make sure Ellie understood he didn't appreciate her matchmaking attempts.

When Jane had first shown up at the restaurant, he'd been prepared to remain closemouthed and unfriendly. The last thing he'd wanted was to give the impression that he was interested in dating some city slicker. Far from it. But soon the beer had loosened his inhibitions and he'd begun to enjoy the lighthearted conversation. He considered Jane's eagerness to adapt to Texas downright charming. When she'd offered to buy a truck to go along with his suggestion for a bumper sticker, he found himself almost taken with her. Damn it, he liked her attitude. Despite appearances, she knew how to have a good time, and as for turning Texan, she was obviously willing to try.

The bill arrived for their dinner and Glen reached for it. "We'll split it," Cal said.

"How much do I owe?" Jane asked, bending down for her purse.

Cal placed his hand on her arm. "It's taken care of."

Ellie beamed him a smile dazzling enough to blind him. He wasn't sure what had made him offer to pay for Jane's dinner. This wasn't a date, wasn't even *close* to one. But hell, he figured he owed the woman that much after the unfriendly way he'd started off the evening.

"What do you want to do now?" Glen asked his wife.

"How about bingo?" Ellie suggested, looking at the others.

"Bingo?" Jane repeated.

"Sure. There's a game every Friday night in the room above the bowling alley," Ellie said. "You'll love it. Just consider it part of your Texas education."

"I...don't think I've ever played," Jane confessed. "But if you think I should..."

"Don't you worry," Cal said, impressed once more with her willingness to fit in. "It's not difficult to learn."

Since the bowling alley was only a couple of blocks away, they decided to walk. Cal wasn't sure why he tagged along. His intent had been to beg off after dinner and join his friends at Billy D's, the local watering hole. Of course Glen wouldn't be around, and probably not Grady, either. Jimmy Morris and Lyle Whitehead would be shooting the breeze as usual—not that Cal was a big fan of Lyle's. The guy was far too ready to take offense and want to settle things with his fists. Anyway, Cal realized that, when it came right down to it, he was enjoying himself with his brother and Ellie. Doc Texas wasn't bad, either, although he was determined to make sure she realized this wasn't a real date.

The upstairs room of the bowling alley was set up with tables and chairs for the twice-weekly bingo sessions. A concession stand in the back of the room sold cold drinks, popcorn and hot dogs. Lloyd Bonney, a retired rancher who'd moved into town a couple of years ago, called out the numbers from his position at the front.

They purchased three bingo cards each and were heading for a table near the electronic bingo board when Cal saw his parents. He groaned inwardly. It would be just like his mother to read far more into their little foursome than was warranted. Mary Patterson refused to accept that her oldest son wasn't interested in marriage. She kept insisting she wanted grandchildren and it was his duty to provide him. Cal was convinced Ellie and his brother would be more than happy to handle that task; he only wished she'd stop harassing *him* about it.

"You want to sit by Mom and Dad?" Glen asked after they'd waved to their parents.

Cal growled his reply and his brother laughed. "That's what I thought."

They located some space at one of the long tables, and the two women ended up sitting between the brothers, which was fine, Cal supposed—although to the casual observer it might look as if Jane was *with* him. He wasn't much of a talker and felt grateful that Ellie and Jane carried on a nonstop conversation. Cal shook his head, amused at the way women could chatter. He never did understand how they could have so much to say to each other.

Lloyd flipped a switch and the electronic board lit up. The air machine bounced the lightweight balls bearing the bingo letters and corresponding numbers.

Because Jane was new to this, Cal watched her cards for her during the first game, checking to be sure she caught the number on each of them.

"B-fifteen," Lloyd called.

Cal checked his own card and closed off the appropriate box. The other two didn't have fifteen in the B row. Once again he glanced over at Jane's row of cards and saw that she'd missed one. He pointed it out to her.

"Oh, thanks," she said, and smiled her appreciation.

A smile. Just a smile, and yet it warmed his heart. He was startled by his reaction. It was so...unexpected. Damn it, something must be wrong with him to take a smile, a simple expression of thanks, and make more of it than was warranted. Obviously he'd had one too many beers.

The evening wore on, and while Cal didn't have any luck, Glen bingoed once for a twenty-five-dollar purse. The last game was the grand finale, Blackout Bingo, where every number on the card had to be closed in order to win the two-hundred-dollar grand prize.

As he had all evening, Cal glanced over at Jane's cards after he'd checked his own numbers. Other than that one time, she hadn't missed any. Lloyd had called out forty-five numbers or so when he noticed that one of Jane's cards was nearly filled. She had four blank spaces compared to his best one, which showed at least ten. The next two numbers Lloyd called were both on Jane's card.

He could feel her excitement growing. Five numbers later she had only one open space. She needed O-sixty-four. Jane closed her eyes, propped her elbows on the table and crossed the fingers on both hands.

Two numbers later Lloyd called, "O-sixty-four."

Together Cal and Jane screamed, "BINGO!"

Cal hadn't meant to yell, but he was damn near as excited as Jane. She leaped to her feet and hugged Ellie and then Cal, as though this two hundred dollars was two hundred thousand.

"Congratulations," Cal said. He couldn't help being delighted. Jane's excitement was contagious.

"Two hundred dollars," she breathed, as if this was more than she'd seen in her entire life. Lloyd personally counted out the money, placing the bills in her hand.

Clutching them in her fist, Jane wildly hugged Ellie again.

Ellie laughed. "I told you that you'd like this game."

"I *love* this game." Jane pressed the money to her heart. "I'm gonna buy me a real Texas outfit. You want to come along and make sure I get what I need?"

"You're on," Ellie replied as Jane tucked the money into her purse.

Afterward Cal and Glen stopped and greeted their parents.

"Mom, Dad, this is my friend Jane Dickinson," Ellie said, saving Cal the embarrassment of introducing her and then explaining that technically she wasn't his date. He was grateful that Ellie had taken the initiative; otherwise his parents might get the wrong idea. His mother didn't need any encouragement to match him up.

"Good to see you dating again," his father said, blindsiding him.

He'd expected his mother to comment on Jane's being with him, but not his father. "This isn't a date," Cal felt obliged to correct him, and not entirely for his dad's sake, either. It saved Jane the need to correct his father's assumption.

"Congratulations on your win, Jane," Mary said. It was easy to read what his mother was thinking— from the look in her eyes, she was already envisioning grandchildren.

After exchanging pleasantries and saying goodbye to his parents, they walked back to the Chili Pepper where they'd left their vehicles. Glen opened the truck door for Ellie and helped her in.

"I had a wonderful time," Jane said, her blue

eyes bright with pleasure. "My best since moving here. Thanks so much for including me."

"How're you getting home?" Glen asked when he apparently realized she hadn't come in a car.

"I walked. It's only a few blocks."

"Would you like a ride?" he asked. Cal probably would have offered but was pleased that his brother had done it first. If Glen hadn't, he'd be obliged, and he didn't want her to think he was seeking out her company.

"I appreciate the offer, but I feel like walking. Thank you, though."

Glen climbed into his truck and backed out of the parking space as Ellie waved farewell.

Cal opened his pickup door, prepared to leave himself. "Sure you don't want a ride?" he said, trying not to sound reluctant.

"Positive. Good night, and thanks for dinner. That was really sweet of you."

Cal stood waiting by the open door until Jane had crossed the main intersection. Only then did he climb into his truck and start the engine. Checking the rearview mirror for traffic, he caught sight of Jane ambling down the street. He sighed, silently cursing himself. He didn't feel right leaving her to walk home on her own. She might not be his date or even his friend, but damn it all, he felt responsible for her safety. Especially when she was walking around with her bingo winnings in her purse. Promise didn't have a crime problem, but it didn't hurt to be cautious.

Cal cut the engine and climbed out of his truck, then raced after her.

She glanced up at him in surprise when he reached her. "I'll walk you home," he said gruffly, matching his steps to hers.

She blinked as if she wasn't sure what to say. "Thank you."

He shoved his fingers into the small pockets at the top of his jeans. They walked in silence, neither of them making an effort to talk. Two blocks off Main Street, Cal was glad he'd decided to escort her home. The streetlight on Fourth Avenue had burned out, and the sidewalk was darker than a bowl of black bean soup.

"Perhaps you'd better give me your arm," Cal suggested halfway down the block.

She did, and he tucked her hand in the crook of his elbow. Oddly, he *enjoyed* doing this small thing for her.

"That's something you and Ellie and Glen forgot to mention," Jane said suddenly.

"What's that?"

"The men in Texas are real gentlemen."

"My momma didn't raise no Bubbas," Cal said, joking, and they both laughed. It felt good to laugh, and Cal had done more of that in the past few hours than he had in months.

"Listen," he said impulsively as they neared the small house behind the health clinic, "are you serious about learning to ride?"

"Very much so."

"All right, then I'll teach you."

"You will?"

Cal wasn't sure what had prompted the offer, but

since he'd blurted it out, he couldn't very well back down now.

The light from her porch illuminated her face. She looked like the original California girl with her short sun-bleached hair and eyes as blue as the Pacific. Already Cal was calling himself a damned fool and he hadn't even given Jane her first lesson. Maybe someone should offer to give *him* a lesson—on how to keep his stupid mouth shut.

SAVANNAH SMITH had made the appointment to see Dr. Jane Dickinson Tuesday morning. She hadn't been feeling well the past few weeks and thought it was time for a general checkup. Besides, she had her suspicions.

In the past half year her life had undergone a number of drastic changes. First and foremost, she'd met Laredo; they'd fallen in love and were now married. About the time Laredo had come into her life, her brother Richard had reappeared after a six-year absence. Thanks to her influence, Grady had allowed Richard to stay at the ranch, which was more than charitable of him, seeing as their brother had stolen from them—and that Grady's inclination had been to turn him away. Apparently she'd still had some lessons to learn regarding Richard. Painful ones.

Savannah had desperately wanted to believe he'd changed, but then, so had Grady. Against his better judgment, her brother had given Richard opportunity after opportunity to prove himself. In the end, when he disappeared with Grady's truck, it was exactly what she'd learned to expect. Only this time he didn't steal only from them; he'd also charged thousands of dollars' worth of goods and services in town. It was a matter of pride and principle to Grady that those bills be paid.

The merchants in Promise had accepted the charges because of the Westons' good name, and Grady wouldn't let Richard disgrace it or ruin a hundred years of excellent credit. The money had come out of the profits from selling off the herd; it was money that could have been spent in other ways, money that would have benefited the Weston ranch, the Yellow Rose.

Savannah's bout of ill health had started shortly after Richard's sudden departure. She'd done her best to hide it from her husband, but Laredo knew something was wrong because he'd been the one to suggest she make the appointment. Sitting in the examination room now, Savannah silently prayed that the diagnosis was what she suspected.

The door to the examination room opened and Dr. Dickinson walked in. It was a bit unsettling to have a doctor younger than she was. Particulary after all those years of seeing old Doc Cummings.

"Hello," Dr. Dickinson said, smiling. She held out her hand and Savannah shook it. This must be a big-city thing, she thought, because generally women in rural Texas didn't shake hands.

"I'm pleased to meet you," Savannah answered. This was their first actual meeting, although they'd seen each other at various events.

The physician sat down on the chair across from her. "You haven't been feeling well?"

Savannah nodded. "My stomach's been queasy,

usually in the morning and often late in the afternoon, too.''

''Any other symptoms?''

''I'm so tired lately. The other night it was all I could do to stay up past eight, which is ridiculous.''

The doctor made a notation on her chart. ''Anything else?''

''Well...yes. My period's two weeks late.''

This information was written on the chart, as well. ''I understand you were recently married.''

Savannah nodded. ''In June.''

''Are you using any form of birth control?''

Savannah found such talk excruciatingly embarrassing. ''Uh, usually,'' she answered, blushing hotly.

''I'd like to do a urine test,'' the doctor said.

''Okay. So do you think I might be pregnant?''

Dr. Dickinson's answering smile was warm. ''You're showing all the symptoms.''

Savannah let out a deep breath as that confirmation settled over her. Pregnant. So soon? She'd known it was the likely reason for her nausea and tiredness—not to mention the missed period. But... pregnant? Somehow, it didn't seem possible, and yet she supposed it was inevitable considering their haphazard methods of birth control.

After a brief physical examination Savannah provided a urine sample. Waiting for the test results seemed to take forever when in reality it was only minutes. Savannah's emotions ran the entire spectrum. She felt mostly an overwhelming sense of joy—a joy so deep and profound it was difficult not to leap up and shout with it. Simultaneously she was aware that the timing could hardly be worse. She and Laredo had spent much of the summer drawing up plans for their own home. Every penny they'd managed to pull together had gone into the project. Now wasn't exactly the ideal time to announce she was going to have a baby.

The door opened and the doctor returned. "Congratulations, Savannah. You're going to be a mother."

Savannah's hands flew to her mouth and tears welled in her eyes.

"How do you feel about this pregnancy?" the physician asked.

"I...it's a surprise. I mean, it is and it isn't. I realize it shouldn't be, but..." She realized she was babbling. "I'm happy. Very happy."

"I'd like to set up a series of appointments for you, plus I'd like to start you on a regimen of vitamins."

"All right."

"Good," Dr. Dickinson said. "So I'll see you in a month." Then she gently patted Savannah's back and left to attend to the next patient.

Savannah's head continued to buzz as she drove back to the ranch. To her amazement Laredo was waiting for her when she pulled into the yard. He hurried over to the truck and opened the door the second she'd parked.

"What did the doctor have to say?" he asked before she had time to climb out. His eyes revealed his anxiety.

"Oh, Laredo, you aren't going to believe this. We're pregnant!"

"Pregnant?"

"Oh, please tell me you're glad. Because I am. I swear I could explode!"

They walked into the kitchen and Laredo pulled out a chair and sat down. "Pregnant," he said again, as if he couldn't quite believe it.

Savannah nodded, studying this man she loved beyond all reason. As she knew it would, a slow easy smile spread across his face. "Pregnant," he said more loudly this time. "My wife's going to have a baby! Just wait until my mother hears about this."

Savannah smiled. Their love was the most profound wonder of her life. And as she'd now discovered, it was only the beginning.

Her husband leaped to his feet and caught her in his arms. "We're going to have a baby!"

"I know the timing's bad..."

"The timing's perfect. You're perfect. Life's perfect." He threw back his head and laughed, and then he kissed her.

"Hey, you two," Grady said when he stepped into the kitchen. "What's going on?"

Chapter Three

For the first time since Jane had come to Texas, she felt a sense of belonging. Friends made all the difference. Her evening out with Ellie, Glen and Cal had cheered her immensely, and within a few days she'd followed all their instructions. She had a Texas bumper sticker, a Willie Nelson cassette in her car, and she routinely listened to the Brewster country-and-western station. A shopping spree with her bingo winnings plus a chunk of her savings had netted her an outfit Annie Oakley would've been proud to wear. Not only that, her first riding lesson was scheduled for Friday afternoon. If she got any more Texan, she wouldn't recognize herself!

Thursday-afternoon traffic in the clinic was slow; she hadn't seen a patient in more than two hours. Attaching her beeper to her waistband, she headed toward Dovie's antique shop, taking the rag doll Maggie Daniels had brought her. Every time she entered the office the old-fashioned doll smiled at her with its faded pink lips, looking somehow forlorn, as though it—she—wanted to pour out her sawdust heart. If anyone could help Jane locate the doll's rightful owner, it was Dovie.

Her friend seemed to be experiencing a lull in business, too. Dovie's face broke into a welcoming smile when Jane walked into the shop.

"Jane, how are you?" Dovie asked, rushing over to hug her. She had to skirt wooden tables and dressers and chairs, all draped and dangling with jewelry and scarves. Jane was impressed by the quantity and quality of Dovie's wares.

"I'm terrific," she answered.

Her arm around Jane's waist, Dovie led her to the Victorian Tea Room and poured them each a cup of fragrant lemon tea. When she'd finished, she asked about Friday night's dinner.

Jane talked nonstop for ten minutes, relating the highlights of the evening. She mentioned winning at bingo and that Cal had walked her home and volunteered to teach her to ride.

"Cal?" Dovie sounded shocked. "Cal Patterson?"

"I know. I was surprised myself. At first I could tell he wasn't thrilled to be paired up with me. He seemed to think I'd finagled this matchmaking myself, but after a while, he was fine." She grinned. "You could say he underwent an attitude adjustment." She considered Cal a gentleman in an age when chivalry was all but dead. He'd gone out of his way to escort her home, out of regard for her safety. That certainly hadn't been required, but Jane appreciated it. In the days since, she'd thought quite a lot about him.

Dovie's eyes twinkled with delight. "You're exactly what that young man needs."

"I met his parents, too."

"Mary and Phil are two of my dearest friends," Dovie told her.

Jane sipped her tea, then lifted the bag with the doll onto her lap. "Actually I have a reason for stopping by other than to let you know how everything went last Friday." She opened the bag and carefully withdrew the fragile toy.

Dovie's eyes widened when she saw it. "Where in heaven's name did you find that?"

Jane hesitated. "I'm not at liberty to say."

Dovie's brows rose a fraction of an inch.

"I will tell you that someone brought it to me—feeling a lot of guilt. Apparently this person took the doll and shouldn't have, and for reasons I can't understand is unable to return it. I was hoping you might know who the rightful owner is."

Dovie turned the antique in her hands and thoroughly examined how it was constructed. "I'd swear it's authentic."

"You mean this *is* a real antique?" Jane asked, wondering where and how six-year-old Maggie could have come by it.

"She's real, and probably worth quite a lot of money."

"You're joking." The doll was ready to fall apart.

"I'm not." Dovie gave the toy back to Jane with some hesitation. "Are you sure you can't tell me the name of the person who gave you the doll?"

Jane shook her head. "I wish I could, but I'd be breaking a confidence."

Dovie accepted her answer. "Do you have any idea where this unnamed person got the doll?"

"Didn't say." In retrospect, Jane realized there were any number of questions she should have asked Maggie. But the child had been in quite a state, sick with regret and worry. At the time it'd seemed more important to reassure the little girl than to worry about the doll's owner.

"There's only one place I can imagine finding anything like this," Dovie said, her look thoughtful. A frown slowly formed, furrowing her brow.

"Where's that?" Jane asked.

"It doesn't seem possible...but there's been talk about it lately and I have to wonder. The doll might have come from...Bitter End."

It was Jane's turn to lift her eyebrows. She'd never heard of the town and was fairly certain she would have remembered one with such an unusual name. "Bitter End?"

"That's the name the settlers chose more than 130 years ago, after the Civil War. If I remember my history correctly, the journey across Indian territory and through the war-ravaged South was harrowing. Not a family came through the trip unscathed. Parents lost children and children lost parents from Indian attacks and disease. By the time they reached the Texas hill country, their faith had nearly been destroyed."

"Times were so difficult back then," Jane said, remembering that the now-common childhood diseases were often the source of death.

"Those pioneers faced hardship after hardship," Dovie continued. "Overcome with bitterness, the town's founding fathers decided to name their community Bitter End.''

"I've never heard of it."

"Few have," Dovie said. "It's a ghost town now."

"Really? You've been there?" Jane asked, her curiosity keen. She'd never dreamed something like that existed in this vicinity.

"Have I been to Bitter End?" Dovie's laugh was abrupt. "I'm sorry to say I haven't. I'd like to and perhaps one day I will. The only reason I even know about it is because of something my father said years ago."

"I'd like to go there," Jane said. She'd always been a history buff, and visiting a ghost town would be a wonderful adventure.

"Jane, I hate to disillusion you," Dovie said kindly, "but I don't even know if the old town is still standing."

"Could you give me directions?"

"If I knew where it was, possibly, but there are no paved roads. It's somewhere up in the hills. You need to remember this is a real ghost town."

"But what happened? Why did everyone leave?" Jane's mind filled with questions.

Dovie looked as though she regretted bringing up the subject. "I don't have a clue. No one does. At one time I believe the town was quite prosperous—a fast-growing community. My father said he'd even heard that the railroad was scheduled to lay track there, but all of that changed overnight."

"Overnight?" The details were becoming more

and more intriguing. "Something drastic must have happened."

"A natural catastrophe, perhaps," Dovie suggested. "No one knows."

"That doesn't make sense," Jane said, thinking out loud. "Tornado, fire, flood—anything like that would have destroyed the whole town. There'd be nothing left. Anyway, why wouldn't they rebuild if that happened?"

"I don't know," Dovie murmured. "My father mentioned it twice in the years I was growing up. As I recall, he said everyone packed up and moved—no one knows why. They abandoned almost everything."

"Then there's a possibility the entire town's intact."

"Yes...I suppose there is," Dovie said.

"Do you know people who've actually been there?"

She took her time answering. "A few."

"Who?"

Dovie was about to speak when the bell above the front door rang, and Sheriff Frank Hennessey walked into the store.

It seemed to Jane that Dovie went pale. "Jane," she whispered, getting to her feet, "don't leave me."

Jane nodded.

"Hello, Sheriff," Dovie said. Her tone lacked its usual warmth.

"Dovie."

The sheriff glanced in Jane's direction, and his look made it clear he wished she wasn't there. In

any other circumstances Jane would have made her
excuses and left, but Dovie had plainly asked her to
stay. However uncomfortable she was, Jane felt
obliged to honor her friend's request.

"What can I do for you, Sheriff?" Dovie asked.

Frank Hennessey glanced at Jane again. "Dovie,
in the name of heaven, this has got to end," he said
in a low urgent voice. "We're both miserable."

"We've already been through this a thousand
times. Nothing's going to change."

The sheriff's mouth thinned. "I love you," he
whispered.

"So you say." Dovie began to move about the
shop, rearranging things here and there. Frank Hennessey trailed behind her, looking lost and utterly
wretched.

When his pleading didn't work, the sheriff tried
a different tactic. "What's this I heard about you
traveling?" he demanded as though he had every
right to know.

"It's time I saw something of the world."

"A *singles'* cruise, Dovie?" His disapproval was
evident.

Dovie sighed expressively. "Who told you?"

"Does it matter?"

"As a matter of fact it does, because I want to be
sure that whoever it was has nothing more to re-
port."

"You didn't want me to know?" The sheriff's
tone had gone from irritated to hurt.

"What I choose to do with my life from here on
out, Frank Hennessey, is *my* concern, and only
mine."

He stiffened. "You don't mean that."

"Yes, Frank, I do." Dovie had completed one full circle of the shop. She stopped in front of the table where she and Jane had been drinking tea. "You remember Dr. Dickinson, don't you?"

The sheriff gave Jane little more than a perfunctory nod.

"Good to see you again, Sheriff Hennessey," Jane said, but she doubted he'd even heard.

His gaze remained on Dovie. "This has gone on long enough," he said, and he no longer seemed to care whether or not Jane was privy to their conversation. "I'm crazy about you. It's been damn near three weeks, and we're no closer to settling this than we were then. I need you, Dovie! It isn't like you to be unreasonable. I don't know who put this craziness in your head, but it's got to end, for both our sakes. Can't we resolve this?"

"Resolve this?" Dovie repeated as if she found the statement amusing. "What you mean is, can't I give in to you. It's not going to happen, Frank. You've made your decision and I've made mine, and that's all there is to it."

"Damn it, Dovie, would you listen to reason?"

"There's nothing more to discuss," Dovie said, not quite disguising the sadness in her tone. "I think it'd be best if you left."

Frank stared at Dovie in disbelief. Then, in an act of pure frustration, he slapped his hat against his thigh and stormed out of the shop, leaving the display windows shaking.

Dovie sank into the chair and Jane noticed that her hands were shaking. "I'm sorry to subject you to that, Jane," she said, her voice as shaky as her hands.

"Are you all right?" Jane asked, truly concerned.

"No," Dovie admitted, "but I will be in time."

"Are you really going away?"

"Yes. I've booked a three-day cruise, but not a singles' one. Mary Patterson suggested that, but I'm not interested in getting involved again—at least not this soon."

"You love Frank, don't you?" Jane probed gently.

"Yes, fool that I am. I do. But he's stubborn, and unfortunately so am I." She didn't elaborate, but Jane had a pretty clear picture of the problem. Dovie wanted a ring on her finger, and Sheriff Hennessey wasn't about to relinquish his freedom. From the looks of it, they were at an impasse.

"You'll enjoy the cruise," Jane said, wanting to encourage her friend in the same kindly way Dovie had encouraged her. "And it'll do you a world of good to get away for a while."

"I'm sure you're right." Dovie made an unsuccessful attempt at a smile. "I talked Mary and Phil Patterson into coming along with me, and by golly, we're going to have the time of our lives."

She said this, Jane noted, as though the person she most needed to convince was herself.

IT CAME AS A SURPRISE to Cal to realize he was actually looking forward to seeing Jane Dickinson again. By Friday afternoon he was ready to teach that California gal everything she cared to know about the joys of riding.

From his brother Cal learned that Ellie and Jane had been shopping and Jane had purchased an entire Western outfit, complete with hat and cowboy boots.

They'd talked briefly by phone earlier in the week, and Cal had suggested Jane come to the ranch at five o'clock, since the days were growing shorter now.

Accustomed to women being late, Cal didn't actually expect her to show up on time. He was pleasantly surprised when her car turned into the yard at five minutes to five.

She parked, then opened the car door and gingerly stepped out. Her clothes were so new they practically squeaked.

"This really is very kind of you," she said, smiling.

Cal walked all the way around her, amazed by the transformation a few clothes could make. She looked great. Terrific. If he didn't know better, he'd have assumed she'd been born and raised in the great state of Texas. At least, until she opened her mouth, and then all doubt was removed. She didn't sound anything like a Texan—but he didn't feel he should hold that against her.

"What do you think?" she asked, holding her arms out at her sides.

"Your Wranglers seem a little stiff, but other than that, not bad. Not bad indeed!"

"Did you check out my bumper sticker?" she asked.

He hadn't, so he turned to look—and roared with laughter. Sure enough, she'd gotten a sticker. It read: *Texas Crude.*

"Not only that, I'm listening to Reba, Clint, John Berry and Alabama."

Cal loved it. "Wonderful."

She laughed and he discovered that he liked the sound of it. Soon he was chuckling himself, and for no damn reason that he could think of. Hmm. Something like this could ruin his reputation as a curmudgeon.

"You ready?" he asked.

"Ready as I'll ever be," she said, then exhaled a deep sigh.

Cal led the way. He'd already chosen Atta Girl for her and brought the horse out of the paddock. Atta Girl was a gentle chestnut mare who'd delivered six foals over the past ten years. Cal trusted her to treat the greenhorn with patience.

"This is Atta Girl," he said, rubbing his hand down the mare's neck.

Jane stood directly in front of the animal. "Pleased to meet you," she said with the same seriousness she might have used to address the bank manager.

"She isn't going to shake your hand," Cal said, struggling not to smile.

Jane gave him a glance that said she didn't find him all that funny, but he noticed she had a hard time containing her amusement, too. It'd been a long time since anyone had affected him this way.

"I thought we'd start with you learning how to saddle her," he said. Once she was familiar with the basics, he'd let her mount.

Jane nibbled her lower lip. "Before I put a saddle

on her back, I thought maybe Atta Girl and I should talk this over.''

He assumed she was joking, but it soon became obvious she wasn't. Apparently she intended to have some polite conversation with Atta Girl first.

"I thought you might like to get a good look at me," Jane said, just as if she were talking to a person. "It must be frustrating to carry someone around without being able to see who it is."

Cal tried not to roll his eyes, but didn't succeed. At this rate it'd take a month of Sundays to get her on Atta Girl's back.

"She can't really see you, anyway," Cal felt honor bound to tell Jane.

"Do you mean to say you gave me a blind horse?"

He shook his head. "Horses are notorious for having bad eyesight. You notice how far apart her eyes are? How they're on either side of her face?"

Jane looked at one side of Atta Girl's face and then the other.

"Because of that, horses have what you might call a broad view of things, and although they can tell when there's something approaching, what they generally see are shadowy figures."

"Oh," Jane said, and tentatively touched the mare's soft muzzle. "In that case, Atta Girl, you need carrots. Lots and lots of carrots. I'll bring you some on my next visit."

"While we're at it," Cal said, "it's probably not a good idea to approach a horse from the rear. It's an ugly way to die."

"How reassuring," Jane muttered.

"Not to worry, you're safe with Atta Girl."

"At least her name isn't something like Killer."

"That was her sire's name," Cal teased.

Jane placed her hands on her hips. "Are you trying to scare me?"

"Would I do something like that?" he inquired, the picture of innocence. While he had her attention, he told her a number of other facts she should know. Riding information, as well as bits and pieces of horse lore. She listened with complete concentration. Not until she'd grown accustomed to riding would she really experience the thrill of it. Nothing in life could compare with galloping through a field of wildflowers on a warm spring day with the wind in your face.

"What kind of relationship do you have with your horse?" she asked. "Do you think of him the way Roy Rogers thought of Trigger?"

"Probably not." He hoped he wasn't shattering any illusions. "Thunder's a loyal partner, but he's not my best friend. The tricks he knows aren't going to end up on any television show, but he cuts cattle better than any pony I've ever ridden." Cal paused, wondering whether to add the next part. "Also, I'm not having him stuffed when he eventually goes."

Jane looked startled, but recovered quickly. She asked a number of intelligent questions, which he answered to the best of his ability.

"You ready to saddle her up?" he asked.

Jane drew a deep breath and nodded.

Having been around horses his entire life, Cal had no fear of them. Respect, yes, but not fear. Jane was intimidated; following his example, though, she refused to show it. Nor would she allow her intimidation to stop her from getting on with the lesson.

Cal brought out the brushes, a blanket, the saddle and tack. He taught her by demonstrating and then letting her do it herself. Atta Girl was everything he'd expected. To his amusement Jane stopped what she was doing several times, walked around to the horse's head and spoke to her. Anyone might have thought they were actually communicating.

"You're sure this isn't too much trouble for you?" she asked Atta Girl next.

"Jane," Cal muttered, thinking she was quite possibly the most sensitive person he'd ever met. Also the most ridiculous, but he found himself more entertained than annoyed.

By the time she had the saddle on, it was close to seven and twilight was beginning.

"We'll save the actual ride for another lesson," he said. "But it'd be a shame if you didn't at least mount her after all this."

Jane's expression was skeptical. "You think I should? Tonight?"

He nodded, then watched as she walked around to discuss the prospect with Atta Girl. "Does she have any objection?" Cal asked as a joke.

"She doesn't seem to," Jane said, apparently taking him seriously.

"I'll help you adjust the stirrups," he said. It was a skill that demanded experience and time. "You're doing great."

"I'll bet that's what they said to Custer before the Battle of Little Big Horn," she complained, then put her foot in the left stirrup and heaved herself up.

Apparently the cinch wasn't as tight as it should have been, because before he could warn her, the saddle slid sideways, sending her directly under Atta Girl's stomach. Jane let out a cry of alarm while Atta Girl pranced about in an effort to maintain her balance. Cal held his breath, fearing the mare would inadvertently step on Jane. To his amazement he watched her roll out from under the horse and leap to her feet. Indiana Jones had nothing on Dr. Texas!

"Are you okay?" Cal asked. Everything had happened so fast he'd barely had time to react. He took hold of Atta Girl's reins and quickly reassured the frightened mare by speaking gently to her.

"That does it," Jane said breathlessly, her hand over her heart.

"You're quitting?" Cal asked, not that he blamed her. She'd had quite a scare.

"No, I'm joining Weight Watchers. I damn near downed that poor horse."

Cal stared at her, then started to chuckle. The laughter came deep from inside him, and nothing could have held it back. Nothing. It was as though two years of fun and laughter had been confined inside him, waiting for precisely this moment. A few hours with Jane Dickinson, and all the pent-up enjoyment of life came spilling out of him in waves of unrestrained delight.

"Well, I'm glad you find this so funny," she said.

Tears ran down his cheeks and he wiped them aside with the back of his hand. "Damn, but I can't remember when I laughed so hard." Jane crossed her arms, and not wanting his reaction to offend her, he gave her a brief hug. "You're a good sport, Jane."

She muttered something unintelligible.

"And listen, there's no need for you to lose weight—you're perfect just the way you are. The saddle slipped because the cinch wasn't tight enough. It had nothing to do with your size."

She seemed none the worse for wear and within seconds she was smiling, too. "You're willing to give me another lesson?"

"You bet, Dr. Texas."

Her smile broadened.

In fact, Cal could hardly wait. This was the most fun he'd had in years. Even Jennifer, the woman he'd loved enough to marry, had never provoked this much reaction in him—apart from the anger and humiliation he felt when she'd dumped him.

"Next week?" Jane asked.

Cal nodded, but waiting an entire week for her second lesson was too long. He wanted to see her again soon.

"Can you make it Tuesday, Dr. Texas?"

She laughed. "You bet, cowboy—and at least my jeans are broken in now."

JANE RETURNED to her house, threw off her clothes and soaked in a hot tub. She couldn't very well claim she was saddle sore, seeing that she hadn't so much as managed to sit on a horse. But she'd taxed rarely-used muscles in her effort to avoid being trampled by Atta Girl.

All Cal had done was laugh, and while he might have been amused, she'd been frightened out of her wits. But all's well that ends well, she decided, not sure if it was the desire to learn to ride or her attraction to Cal that had prompted her to agree to a second lesson.

She liked him. A lot.

Climbing out of the tub, she dressed in a light robe, made some popcorn for dinner and settled down in front of the television with a rented video. The tape had just started when the phone rang.

It was so rare for her phone to ring that she stared at it for a moment. Any emergency calls came through her beeper. At last she picked it up.

"Hello?"

"Janey, it's Mom. How are you, sweetheart?"

"I'm feeling wonderful." She reached for the remote control and stopped the movie. Since her arrival in Promise she'd tried to hide her unhappiness from her parents. Now she was eager to share the good news of making friends and becoming part of the community.

"You sound terrific."

"Listen, honey," her father said, speaking from the extension, "your letter arrived this afternoon. What's all this about a ghost town?"

Excited after her discussion with Dovie, Jane had written home, elaborating on the story, adding bits of speculation and her decision to learn everything she could. From what Dovie had said, the frontier town was real; information had been passed down from one generation to the next. But still, a person could grow up believing in some historical "fact" and later learn it had been a legend with little or no basis in reality.

"Do you honestly believe there's such a place as Bitter End?" her mother asked.

"I don't know, but I'd like to find out."

"How do you intend to do that?" her father wanted to know. "You didn't tell us in your letter."

"I don't know..." Dovie had told her there weren't any roads leading to the ghost town, and a quick survey of an area map revealed a thousand spots where the old town might be.

"I'm as fascinated by all this as you are," her mother said. "I've always loved history, too."

"What interests me is the mystery involved," Jane said.

"You mean why everyone left the town?" her father said.

"Yes. If I understood Dovie correctly, the town was thriving. Then overnight everyone just packed up and moved away. Actually they came here, to Promise."

"And nobody knows why they abandoned one town and founded another," her mother said.

"That's right," Jane said. "No one seems to know. Dovie's never been there herself, but from what she told me there's a good possibility the entire town is still standing."

"But it's over a hundred years old."

"Over 130. As far as I've been able to find out from reading state history, the original settlers were probably a mixed bag of immigrants, outlaws and Southern sympathizers who'd lost everything in the Civil War. That was pretty typical of the people who came to Texas at that time. Most of them had packed up what was left of their worldly belongings and traveled here, hoping to put the war behind them."

"I'm fascinated," her mother said again. "I'll do some research and see if I can find any books that mention Bitter End."

"Thanks, Mom, that'd be great."

"It sounds from your letter," her father said, "that you're enjoying Texas. This last letter was a lot less...reserved than before."

Jane chuckled. "Well, I've got a complete cowgirl outfit now, and one of the local ranchers calls me Dr. Texas."

It was her father's turn to chuckle. "Don't let him give you any ideas. You're Dr. California, understand?"

She did. She was following in her grandfather's and her uncle Ken's footsteps. As soon as her student loans were paid off, she'd be joining her uncle's medical practice in Los Angeles. One day she'd inherit the practice. Uncle Ken claimed she was his favorite niece. While a couple of her cousins had shown an interest in medicine, she was the only one who'd taken it seriously. The schooling had been difficult, her internship and residency demanding. She'd given up every aspect of a social life and been left to deal with a huge debt.

Her parents had helped her out financially, but medical school was expensive. Her uncle had offered to help, too. Still, when the opportunity arose to wipe out most of her debt by working in Texas, she'd leaped at the idea. Three years was nothing. The time would pass before she knew it, or so she'd believed.

Her first six months in Promise had proved otherwise.

Until recently.

Until she met Cal Patterson.

Chapter Four

Late Monday night Frank sat in his patrol car outside Dovie Boyd's home, mulling over what he should do next. He was miserable, and he knew she was, too. He'd loved Dovie for a lot of years, but this was the first time he'd encountered her stubbornness. It was enough to drive a man to drink.

Louise Powell, dressed to the hilt in her Texas trash, complete with star-shaped sunglasses and a silvery hat with a rhinestone band, had approached him at the bowling alley café. She'd let it drop that Dovie had booked a singles' Caribbean cruise. Now if that didn't beat all. Louise had gotten the information from Gayla Perkins at the travel agency and had taken great delight in rubbing his nose in it.

It was downright embarrassing. Here was the town gossip, flapping her tongue all over the county, telling everyone who cared to hear that Dovie was seeking greener pastures.

His fingers tightened around the steering wheel as he reviewed his options. He'd tried, heaven knew he'd tried, but damn it all, he loved Dovie and he didn't want to lose her, especially to another man.

He checked his wristwatch and knew she hadn't gone to bed yet. He sighed deeply, remembering the times they'd cuddled up together on her big feather bed, watching television. She'd made the everyday routines of life special, adding her own little touches here and there. She sun-dried the bed sheets, then stored them with woven lavender wands so that when he crawled in beside her he felt their cool crispness and breathed in the light perfumed scent of summer.

Dinner, too, was something special. Dovie set her table with a linen cloth and napkins, using china and real crystal. She could serve home-baked macaroni and cheese with the panache of the finest restaurant.

Damn, but he missed her.

Swallowing his pride, Frank stepped out of the car and approached the house. He had to try one last time. If he couldn't get her to listen to reason tonight, then he'd have no choice but to accept her decision.

As was his habit, he parked the car around the corner, out of sight from the street, and approached through the backyard. He missed their night together more than he would've thought possible. He knew Dovie, and she was lusty and vital, a real woman with a woman's needs. It was a source of consolation to realize she must miss their nights together, too.

He knocked lightly on the back door and waited, hat in hand.

The porch light went on and he saw her pull aside the lace curtain and peek out. It was several long seconds before she unlocked the door and opened it.

"Hello, Dovie." He kept his gaze lowered. Coming to her like this wasn't easy.

"Frank."

He didn't speak, but merely raised his eyes to hers. He loved her, as much as he was capable of loving any woman. Surely she knew that! But he wasn't the marrying kind. He couldn't help it; he needed his freedom in order to breathe. Marriage, even to Dovie whom he adored, would feel like a noose around his neck.

Everything had been perfect. They'd each had their own lives and a life together, too. He had his house and she had hers. Two nights a week he joined her for mutual pleasure. He was willing to do whatever it took, short of marriage, to return to that arrangement.

"It's not true," she said, breaking the silence, "about the singles' cruise. I don't know who told you that, but I'm not looking for another man."

A weight seemed to lift from his shoulders. So she wasn't seeking out someone else. Although he was grateful, all he could manage was a nod.

"I've just decided to do some traveling," she told him.

"Why?" That was another thing he'd always loved about Dovie—she enjoyed the simple pleasures in life. She shunned luxuries, content with a walk in the moonlight when he would gladly have taken her out for an evening at a fancy restaurant.

"I've lived my entire life in Promise," she explained. "If I don't travel now, I never will. I understand the Caribbean is lovely and I've always dreamed of visiting the islands there. At one time I thought I'd see it with—''

"I'll take you." If all she wanted was a trip, a vacation away, he'd book their passage in the morning. No questions asked. Anywhere in the world she wanted to go.

"As your wife, Frank?"

The bubble of hope he'd felt burst with her words. "Oh, Dovie, you know I can't do that."

"Yes, I do know. That's why I'll be traveling without you."

The frustration was almost intolerable. "Don't you miss me?" he cried. He ached with the need to hold her.

She looked away but not before he saw the sheen of tears in her eyes.

"I miss you so much," she whispered.

"Oh, Dovie." He reached for her hand and kissed her palm. "Can't we work this out like two adults? I love you and you love me. It's all we need, all we've ever needed."

Her skin was silky smooth and touching it fired all his love, all his passion. "Let me spend the night." His eyes pleaded with her.

Her long hesitation gave him hope.

"No," she finally whispered.

"Dovie, you don't mean that!"

"I do mean it." She eased her hand from his grasp.

Frank couldn't believe this was happening. He'd come so close to convincing her—and he wasn't about to give up without a fight.

"I'm a man with strong needs," he said, hoping that would influence her.

"I love you, but I'm not sleeping with you again, Frank, not unless we're married."

"Dovie." He groaned her name. Damn it, the time had come to play hardball, acquaint her with a few facts. "There are other women in Promise who'd welcome my attention." He was a handsome cuss and he knew it, but there wasn't a woman in the world he wanted more than Dovie Boyd.

"Yes, I'm sure any number of them would," Dovie said.

Frank saw the hurt in her eyes and was furious with himself for suggesting he'd consider seeing anyone else. But he'd tried everything possible to get her to listen to reason.

"Perhaps another woman *would* be the best answer," Dovie murmured. She stepped back from the threshold.

He opened his mouth to tell her he'd been only bluffing, but he wasn't given the opportunity. Dovie's door was closed firmly in his face. He stared at it in stunned silence.

Hell and damnation, the woman drove him crazy! It'd serve her right if he did go out with someone else. Maybe then she'd realize what she was giving up; maybe then she'd come to her senses. Yup, that was what he'd do, Frank decided. She was taking a fancy cruise and plenty of eligible men were bound to come sniffing around. Well, he was entitled to some compensations, too.

Eventually, he hoped she'd accept that, even though he loved her with all his heart, he wasn't about to let her or any other woman maneuver him into marriage. In a few months he'd be sixty-one years old. He'd managed to avoid marriage so far. Why would he change now? Marriage was a trap, especially for a man like him—despite those sentimental beliefs of Dovie's.

But as soon as she learned he was seeing another woman, she'd be back. What had begun as a bluff now sounded like a good strategy. Dovie needed some competition; that way she'd realize how good they'd had it. One thing about Dovie, she was a fast learner.

Frank felt another faint stirring of hope. Before long, he told himself, Dovie would be begging him to come back.

EARLY TUESDAY AFTERNOON Ellie stepped outside the feed store and inserted a few coins in the pop machine. The morning had been hectic and she was grateful for this respite, however brief. She opened the can of soda and saw Jane Dickinson walking across the street.

"Jane," she called, raising her hand in greeting. "Come on over."

Jane returned the wave, glanced both ways, then crossed the street.

Ellie's father had recognized early in his career the importance of customer relations. He'd strived to make the feed store a friendly place in which to conduct business. He'd wanted to give ranchers and anyone else who dropped off an order a cozy place to sit and chat. The large shaded porch had been furnished with chairs and a pop machine for that purpose.

She and Glen had spent many an afternoon in this very spot. They'd been friends long before they'd fallen in love—a love it took them far too long to recognize or acknowledge. Even now, a month after their wedding, it astonished her that they could have been so blind to their feelings.

"Hi," Ellie greeted Jane. "I heard about the riding lesson," she said carefully.

Jane smiled and claimed an empty seat beside Ellie. "It went okay—I think. Cal's teaching me with Atta Girl, and other than damn near toppling the mare, I did fine."

Glen had told Ellie the story of the saddle slipping during Jane's first lesson. He reported that Cal had laughed so hard in his telling of the story he was almost incomprehensible. It'd taken Glen a while to understand what had happened.

"Actually I'm amazed you're willing to go back for a second lesson, seeing the way Cal behaved," Ellie said, wanting to kick her brother-in-law for his lack of manners.

At the mention of his name, Jane's face brightened. "He was great," she said. "Patient and gentle."

Ellie wondered if she was having a hearing problem. It wasn't possible that they were referring to the same person. *"Cal?"*

Jane eyed her. "Yes, Cal. He's the one who's teaching me."

"I've never heard him referred to as patient and

gentle, at least not since Jennifer—'' Ellie stopped abruptly.

"Who's Jennifer?" Jane asked.

Ellie sighed inwardly. She'd already mentioned Cal's former fiancée so she might as well continue. "She and Cal were...friendly at one time."

"Friendly?"

"An item."

"How much of an item?"

Ellie could see there was no help for it. "They were engaged."

Jane didn't respond right away. "I see."

Ellie wouldn't have said another word if Jane hadn't pressed. Would have preferred it that way. Apparently Cal was quite taken with the new doctor, and she didn't want to be responsible for upsetting this hopeful turn of events.

"Do you mind telling me what happened?"

That was difficult. If this had concerned anyone other than Cal, Ellie would have suggested Jane simply ask him. But for the past two years Cal had closed himself off from most people as a result of the broken engagement. And he'd rejected the possibility of any other relationship with a woman. Ellie didn't want to scare Jane off; if anything she wanted to encourage a romance between these two lonely people.

Glen had been shocked when he learned that Cal had offered to teach Jane to ride. Even Ellie had been surprised. And delighted. Naturally she'd *hoped* he'd volunteer, but she'd believed it'd take some champion finagling on her part. The last thing she'd expected was for Cal to volunteer on his own.

Ellie hesitated, wondering how much she should say. "There isn't really that much to tell."

"I don't mean to pry," Jane said.

"Well...you should probably know," Ellie said. "Cal never did tell us exactly what went wrong. He loved Jennifer. Anyone looking at the two of them could see the way he felt about her."

Jennifer, though, wasn't the type Ellie would have chosen for her brother-in-law, but then, Cal hadn't sought her opinion. Glen hadn't been impressed by Jennifer, either, but like Ellie, had kept his views to himself. Ellie had met Jennifer, who'd worked at a local branch of a large bank, in the course of business. She'd quickly decided Jennifer Healy was selfish and manipulative, an opinion shared by a number of other people Ellie knew.

"I gather they disagreed about something, and two days before the wedding," Ellie continued, "Jennifer called the whole thing off. She gave him back the ring and left town."

"Moved?"

"To Houston. Glen heard sometime later that she was living with a salesman."

"She walked out two days before the wedding," Jane repeated slowly.

"A big family wedding," Ellie elaborated. "Cal was stuck with phoning all the guests and telling them the wedding was off. He had to return gifts, cancel all the arrangements... Humiliating, huh? Naturally, everyone speculated about what had gone wrong. But Cal didn't want to answer questions, so he retreated. Didn't come into town for months."

"It must have been a painful time for him."

Ellie nodded. "He wasn't the same afterward."

Jane's eyes asked the obvious question although she didn't voice it.

Ellie answered it, anyway. "He likes you, Jane. You know something? In two years you're the first woman he's done more than speak a few gruff words to."

"Me?" Jane flattened her palm against her chest.

"Yes. I know I'm right. He likes you."

Jane laughed and shook her head. "I don't think so."

"He's teaching you to ride, isn't he?"

"Yes, but I suspect that's because he felt sorry for me."

Ellie dismissed the excuse with a shake of her head. "You don't know Cal the way I do. Since Jennifer walked out on him, his attitude toward women has been less than charitable. Trust me, he's interested in you."

WITH ELLIE'S WORDS ringing in her ears, Jane headed out to Lonesome Coyote Ranch for her second riding lesson. It'd been four days since her last one and she was looking forward to learning more. About horseback riding, yes, but also about Cal Patterson.

Ellie had said it'd been two years since Cal's broken engagement. Two years since he'd participated in anything social. What her friend didn't know was that it'd been even longer for Jane. She was twenty-eight years old and couldn't remember her last real date. There'd been a few get-togethers with other medical students, but even these had been severely curtailed during her internship and residency. When it came to dating, high-school girls had more experience and finesse than she did.

Cal was already in the yard when she arrived. "Howdy," he greeted her.

"Hi." She walked away from her parked car. As she'd jokingly said on Friday, her jeans were less stiff this time. The boots, however, still felt awkward, but eventually she'd get used to wearing them, or so Max Jordan had assured her.

Cal's smile was warm. "I wasn't sure you'd show."

"Why not?"

He chuckled. "Ellie tells me it was exceptionally rude to laugh at your, uh, accident. She says I should apologize."

Jane shrugged off his apology, such as it was. "I'm willing to put the incident behind us if you are."

"I am." He led the way toward the barn. "Atta Girl's been waiting for you. She'd like a second chance, too."

The first part of the lesson went well, as they reviewed what she'd learned the last time. She saddled Atta Girl herself, making sure to check the cinch, then mounted the mare with a boost from Cal and a minimum of fuss.

"How does it feel?" he asked, taking the reins and leading Atta Girl into the corral.

"I didn't realize I'd be this high off the ground." She gripped the saddle horn with both hands. Once they arrived at the fenced area, Cal gave her the reins, and Jane held on for dear life.

Cal had her ease Atta Girl forward in a slow walk. Not bad, she decided. In fact, it was kind of exciting.

"This is great!" she called out. Some of her excitement must have communicated itself to Atta Girl, because the mare increased her speed.

"Ride the horse, not the saddle," he reminded her.

"I know," she shouted back. His advice, however, did little good. Try as she might, Jane felt her rear bouncing hard on the unyielding saddle. She'd bounce up and slam down against the leather with a force powerful enough to jar her molars. Fearing she was about to lose her hat, she held on to it with one hand.

"Are you sure I'm doing this right?" she shouted to Cal, certain she wouldn't be able to maintain her balance another minute. The ground looked a long way down.

Cal mounted his own horse and rode next to her, circling the corral. She envied the grace with which he rode; it was as if man and beast moved as one, just the way those cowboy books said. Jane attempted to work her body in unison with Atta Girl's movements, but couldn't find the appropriate rhythm, despite her efforts.

"How...am...I...doing?" Each word vibrated as she rebounded against the saddle.

"You're a natural," Cal assured her. He slowed the gelding's pace and Atta Girl followed suit. Jane's rear end was grateful, not to mention the rest of her. She would never have guessed that her *teeth* would hurt after a riding lesson.

"Will I ever feel as comfortable in a saddle as

you?'' she asked, envying his skill and grace. She marveled that he hadn't so much as worked up a sweat.

"Give it time," he said.

Together, side by side, they circled the corral, keeping to a walk. By the time Cal guided her to the gate and helped her dismount, she'd begun to feel like a real rider.

Except for the fact that her legs almost went out from under her when her boots touched the ground. She waited for the numbness to fade, adjusted her jeans and took her first steps. Once she was assured that her teeth were intact and her head wasn't in danger of falling off, she was able to talk.

"I hurt less after a forty-mile bicycle ride," she said, rubbing her derriere with both hands.

"You're still a tenderfoot."

"It isn't my feet that are tender," she countered.

Cal threw back his head and laughed, although she didn't think she'd been that funny. "I don't know anyone who makes me laugh the way you do," he said.

"I just speak the truth," she muttered, and he laughed again.

He helped her remove the saddle and rub down Atta Girl, then invited her to the house.

For a bachelor's place, the house was meticulous. The kitchen countertops were spotless. Either he didn't cook or he cleaned up after himself. Judging by the guys she'd known in medical school, he was a rare man if it was the latter.

"Thirsty?" he asked, opening the refrigerator. "Want a drink?"

"Please."

He took out a couple of cans of soda and handed her one. They sat at the kitchen table, Jane wincing as her rear end made contact with the hard wooden seat.

"You doing anything Friday night?" Cal asked casually, then took a deep swallow of soda.

"Nothing important," she said, thinking he was asking about her next riding lesson. "What time would you like me to be here?"

"Here?" He frowned. "I was inviting you to dinner."

At first Jane was too stunned to answer. Cal Patterson was asking her out on a date. A real date. It'd been so long since she'd been asked that she didn't even recognize it when she was. "I'd be—" she flashed him a smile "—delighted. I'll look forward to seeing you Friday night."

When he walked her to her car a few minutes later, he told her that her riding was progressing nicely.

She grinned. "That's because I've got a great teacher."

Cal opened her car door. "I'll pick you up at seven," he said. "That okay?"

"Seven," she agreed, and hoped he didn't hear the nervousness in her voice. She had a *date*, a real date. With Cal Patterson.

Maybe Texas wasn't so bad, after all.

FRIDAY NIGHT Cal shifted the hangers from one side of his closet to the other, looking for a decent shirt.

He didn't know what in hell had prompted him to invite Jane to dinner.

Then again, he *did* know. He liked her. Fool that he was, he'd allowed her to get under his skin. He blamed Ellie for this. Blamed and thanked, depending on how he felt at any given moment.

He could add Grady Weston's name to the list of troublemakers. First, his brother decides to marry Ellie. Then not a month passes before Cal's best friend from childhood announces *he's* engaged, too. Grady was going to marry Caroline Daniels, the postmistress. Cal shook his head. The men in Promise were deserting bachelorhood in droves.

Cal had no intention of joining their ranks. Asking Jane to dinner might be misconstrued as romantic interest in the town's new doctor, but that wasn't the case. He liked her, enjoyed her company, but considered her safe. She was a California girl, born and raised. A city girl. In three years' time, she'd be heading back where she belonged, where she fit in. What appealed to him was the way she could make him laugh. And hell, stuck as she was in small-town Texas, he felt sorry for her.

That was it, Cal decided as he jerked a clean shirt off the hanger and put it on. He knew she was all alone down here; he was just being nice to an out-of-state girl, inviting her to share a meal and a few laughs. After that he wouldn't see her again, he vowed. Except for their riding lessons, of course.

He hadn't actually expected her to show up for the second lesson, not after the way he'd reacted to her fall off the saddle. A smile touched the corners of his mouth as he remembered her Butch Cassidy roll beneath Atta Girl's belly. My, oh my, could that woman move. Which led to thoughts he immediately censored....

He fastened the shirt snaps and eased into a clean pair of Wranglers. He wasn't going to a lot of trouble for this dinner, no sir. Nor had he mentioned it to his brother. Glen would make more of it than was there, and he'd for sure tell his wife. Cal did *not* want Ellie to know about this.

A Johnny Cash tune drifted into his mind and he whistled along—until he realized what he was doing and abruptly stopped. He hadn't whistled in years. What the hell was happening here?

The forty-minute drive into town was accomplished in no time at all, or so it seemed. He'd take Jane to dinner as promised, then the minute they were finished he'd escort her home, head to Billy D's and meet up with his friends. On Friday night Billy's was always packed.

Another thing he'd do, Cal determined as he walked the short distance from the curb to Jane's front door, was have a little heart-to-heart with the doc. He had to explain that while this evening was a pleasant diversion, this was not a relationship with a future. It wasn't a relationship, period.

As gently as he could he'd tell her that he wasn't interested in her romantically. There wasn't any point in it, seeing that she'd be returning to California and he was staying here. Being the kind of guy he was, honest and straightforward, he didn't want to mislead her into believing something could develop out of this. It was just a dinner. One dinner.

He rang her doorbell and waited. He might even say something right away. Get it over with quickly.

The door opened and Cal's jaw dropped. Wow. Jane was beautiful. She wore a two-tone blue denim ankle-length skirt with a matching blouse. The buttons were big silver-dollar coins. With her sparkling blue eyes and short blond hair, she looked sophisticated. Western *and* sophisticated. Sort of L.A. meets San Antonio. It was all he could do not to slobber.

"I'll be ready in a moment," she said, holding open the screen door.

Cal removed his hat when he walked into the small house. He remained standing while she reached for her purse and clipped the beeper onto her black leather belt.

"I'm on call," she said, explaining the beeper.

"You clean up real good," he said once he found his voice.

She smiled. "You don't look so bad yourself."

"Any place special you'd like to eat?" he asked.

"You choose."

Not that there was much choice. The Chili Pepper was the best restaurant in town, but they'd eaten there the week before. The café in the bowling alley served damn good chow, but it wasn't the type of place to take Dr. Texas, especially with her dressed to the nines. That left the Mexican Lindo, which he suggested.

"I'm game," she said.

The restaurant was less than five blocks away and the weather was accommodating, so they walked. They were led to a corner booth and Cal felt grateful for that, since it afforded them a measure of privacy. They'd barely sat down when the waiter delivered a bowl of corn chips and fresh salsa. Jane glanced at the menu and quickly made her decision.

"Cheese enchiladas," she told him before he could ask.

Cal selected chili verde, one of his favorites.

He asked for a beer, and because she was on call, Jane ordered an iced tea. They were just beginning to relax when Jane's beeper went off.

She removed it from her belt and read the code. "There's an emergency," she said. "If you'll wait a couple of minutes, I'll phone the service."

"Sure." This was what he wanted, Cal tried to tell himself. She was offering him a perfect out, and he should be thankful. He hadn't stopped to think about the questions their being together was sure to raise. Lots of questions, especially from his family and friends.

Jane was gone only a couple of moments. "It's Jeremy Bishop," she said, hurrying back. "Nell thinks he's broken his arm. She's driving him to the clinic now."

"Is it bad?"

"I won't know until I see him. I'm sorry, Cal, but I have to go."

"I understand," he assured her.

Her eyes showed her regret before she turned and walked quickly out the door. As soon as she was gone, he realized she'd be alone at the clinic. Nell was an emotionally strong woman, but Jeremy was her son and she might need someone to talk to while Jane dealt with the boy's injury.

Cal signaled the waiter. "Can you bring me the bill?"

The young man was clearly flustered. "But you haven't eaten yet. If there's a problem..."

"There's no problem," Cal said. "Dr. Dickinson had an emergency and I've decided to leave myself."

The waiter nodded gravely. "Your order just came up. Would you like a takeout box?"

"Sure," Cal said. He hadn't thought of that.

When the waiter finished transferring the dinners to cardboard containers, Cal paid for them and made his way to the clinic.

He arrived at the same time as Nell, Jeremy, and Nell's other child, Emma. Nell looked pale and distraught. She'd wrapped Jeremy's arm in a pillow; he was obviously in pain and his face was streaked with tears.

"Hello, Jeremy," Jane said, taking charge immediately.

Cal wasn't sure she realized he was there until she turned. "Oh! Hi, Cal."

"I thought I'd keep Nell company in the waiting room," he said.

"Good idea." She thanked him with a smile. Cal put their dinners on the reception desk and guided Nell to a chair, while Jane slid an arm around Jeremy's shoulders and steered him toward the examination room.

"I want to be with my son," Nell insisted.

"I'll come for you in a few minutes," Jane promised, "but first I need an X ray to see what we're dealing with here."

Nell accepted the decision and sank into her chair. She stared straight ahead, her features sharp with fear. "I found him by the tractor," she whispered.

Cal wasn't sure she was talking to him, but he understood the significance of what she was saying. Nell had been the one to find her husband trapped beneath a tractor. The vehicle had turned over on him and crushed him, and she'd been powerless to do anything but hold his hand while he died.

"Jeremy climbed up on it even though I've warned him repeatedly to stay away."

"Seems to me he's learned his lesson," Cal said. "I don't think you'll have any problem keeping him away from now on."

Nell smiled, and Cal wondered if he should stick around or head over to Billy D's. To his surprise he discovered he had no real desire to join his friends. He'd much rather stay right where he was and help Nell—and Dr. Texas.

Chapter Five

"In a month you'll be husband and wife," Reverend Wade McMillen said, leaning back in his leather chair in the study.

It didn't seem possible, but the wedding date had sneaked up on her. Caroline had discovered that putting together a wedding, even a small one involving just family and a few close friends, had demanded every spare moment she had.

"A month," Caroline repeated, glancing at Grady. They'd been attending counseling sessions with Wade for the past few weeks. Even now, Caroline had a difficult time taking it all in. She'd loved Grady for years, but had hidden her feelings behind a prickly attitude. It used to be they couldn't stay in the same room without sparks flying and tempers flaring. They ignited fireworks now, too, but for other reasons.

"It doesn't seem possible," Grady said, his gaze holding Caroline's.

"You're as ready now as you'll ever be," Wade said, grinning at them. "I've counseled a lot of couples in my time. I often get a feel for the relationship before the vows are spoken. And I'm confident the two of you are going to have a strong secure marriage.''

Grady reached for Caroline's hand and squeezed her fingers. "I feel that way, too."

Caroline nodded, her love for Grady clear to see.

"No problems with Maggie?" Wade asked.

"None." Caroline assured him. There'd been a time when the child had been terrified of Grady's booming voice, but no longer. Her six-year-old was enthralled with him. Caroline had no doubt of his love for her daughter. The day Maggie had disappeared, kidnapped by Richard Weston, Grady had proved how deeply he cared for the child. And for her.

"She isn't showing any bad effects from the time she was missing, then?" Wade went on.

"Not that we can tell," Caroline replied. "She seems to be sleeping better these days. She hasn't woken up with nightmares recently, either." Caroline frowned, shaking her head. "No matter how hard I tried, though, I couldn't get her to tell me about her dreams—or what happened when she was gone. Then overnight, the bad dreams stopped. She's her normal cheerful self again."

"She talks about me becoming her daddy and seems genuinely excited about it," Grady added.

Wade looked at him. "You were worried you were somehow the cause of Maggie's nightmares?"

"Yeah, but now she's more accepting of me and more affectionate than ever."

Caroline nodded; she was pleased that Grady had started the adoption process. "I'm convinced that whatever was troubling her is somehow connected to the time Richard had her."

"Richard," Wade repeated, his brow furrowed. "Has anyone heard anything from him or about him lately?"

"Not a word," Grady said. "I know the sheriff's pretty frustrated. It's like Richard's disappeared off the face of the earth."

A chill raced down Caroline's spine every time she thought about Grady's brother. He'd hurt a lot of people, but what infuriated her more than anything was how he'd used and abused his own family. He'd run off with the ranch assets the day the Westons laid their parents to rest, creating untold hardship for Grady and his sister, Savannah. Six years later he'd returned, down on his luck. Grady and Savannah had taken him back in, tried to help him, and once more Richard had proved he couldn't be trusted. After charging thousands of dollars' worth of goods, Richard had disappeared again.

Grady, being honorable and decent, had paid those bills himself rather than have the local businesses absorb the losses. While it meant they wouldn't be starting their marriage with any substantial savings, Caroline loved Grady for being the kind of man he was.

"Shall we schedule the wedding rehearsal?" Wade asked.

Brimming with excitement, Caroline and Grady nodded; soon after, their session was over.

Grady tucked his arm around her waist as they left the church and headed toward the parking lot.

"Have I told you today how much I love you?"

Grady asked. He kissed her as he opened the passenger door.

"It's something I'm not going to tire of hearing," Caroline said. Grady's love was a blessing she hadn't expected to receive. She was coming to this marriage with a child and a lot of emotional baggage. Much of that was thanks to Richard, who'd fathered Maggie during a brief and ultimately meaningless liaison. So meaningless he didn't even remember it. Caroline had been terrified that this would make her and Maggie a burden for Grady, another mess of Richard's he had to clean up. She'd been convinced it would be better to let Grady walk out of her life—but he'd refused to let that happen. He loved her and Maggie. When she told him about Maggie's father, his initial reaction had been shock—because she'd kept the truth from him. But he'd recovered quickly and said that the man who raised and loved Maggie would be her *real* father, and that would be him. In the weeks since their engagement Grady had proved his devotion to her and to Maggie over and over again.

"Do we need to pick up Maggie right away?" Grady asked now.

Dovie Boyd had volunteered to baby-sit the little girl during the counseling sessions with Wade. "What do you have in mind?" she asked, leaning her head against his shoulder.

Grady started the truck's engine. "I was thinking we could stop at the bowling alley for a pizza." He glanced at her. "You game?"

"I'm game for anything with you," she assured

him. "But I'll need to phone Dovie to make sure Maggie's okay first."

"No problem." He backed out of their parking space and they drove to the bowling alley.

After a quick phone call, Caroline joined Grady in a booth at the café. He got out so she could slip in beside him. Not so long ago, he'd have preferred to sit in the cold rather than share her company, Caroline mused. Now they could hardly bear to be separated by even a table.

"Everything all right with Maggie?" he asked.

"She's fine. Dovie said she's already asleep."

"Hey, first grade is a big step for a kid."

Especially when Maggie had only recently outgrown naps. She fell asleep before her eight o'clock bedtime most evenings.

"Dovie doesn't mind keeping her a bit longer?"

"Not at all," Caroline told him. She didn't mention that she was worried about her friend. Although Dovie hadn't said much about her breakup with Sheriff Hennessey, it had obviously been hard for her; a smile didn't come as easily and she seemed listless, depressed. From what Caroline had seen of the sheriff, he wasn't handling the situation any better.

Caroline wished she could help in some way, but experience had taught her that Frank and Dovie had to work this out themselves. She wasn't optimistic, though. Their relationship had been a long-standing one, and if they were going to reconcile, she suspected it would have happened by now.

"I talked to Glen yesterday and he told me something about Cal," Grady said after they'd ordered the mushroom-and-pepperoni pizza. "You'll never guess."

"When it comes to Cal, you're right—I won't guess."

"He's got a date."

"A date? Cal?" Caroline was shocked. "Who?"

Grady smiled. "The new doc."

"Jane Dickinson?"

"Right. He's teaching her how to ride."

This *was* news. "What possessed him to do such a thing? Cal, the woman-hater."

Grady shrugged. "Hell if I know. I gotta tell you it came as a shock to me, too." He leaned toward Caroline. "Cal didn't even tell his brother. Glen found out from his mother, who heard about it from Dovie, who heard from the good doctor herself."

"Typical," Caroline said with a laugh. "But still, it sounds promising."

Love would change Cal Patterson, and she was anxious to see it happen. Ever since his broken engagement, he'd shut himself off from any association with the opposite sex. Caroline suspected falling in love would have a positive powerful impact on him.

Caroline liked Cal and knew that his friendship was important to Grady. She was pleased that Grady had asked him to serve as best man at their wedding. In every way that counted, Cal was more of a brother to Grady than his own.

"I saw Cal's truck this evening," Grady said.

"Parked outside the health clinic," Caroline guessed.

He nodded. "I have a feeling about this."

"A good feeling, I hope."

"A very good feeling," he said, grinning.

THE CLOCK SAID almost ten before Jane had finished setting Jeremy Bishop's arm and securing it in a cast. After giving Nell instructions for the pain medication, Jane and Cal walked the family outside.

"You were a good patient, Jeremy," Jane told the boy. He'd been in a lot of pain, but despite that, he'd willingly cooperated with everything she'd needed him to do.

"He's got a lot of his father in him," Nell said, looking proudly at her son. She stood outside her car, drawn and tired from the ordeal. "Thank you both," she said. "I was pretty shaken when we first arrived. I'm afraid if I'd gone into the examination room, I'd have done something stupid—like faint."

Jane had thought the same thing. "You're his mother. It's to be expected."

"You were great with him," Nell told her. "I can't thank you enough."

"That's what I'm here for." It was helping people like Nell and her family that made Jane's job a pleasure. They hadn't really met before tonight, but she'd heard about Nell from Ruth Bishop, a heart patient. Nell was a widow and Ruth's daughter-in-law.

"Go home, get plenty of rest, and if the pain doesn't decrease, give me a call."

"I will," Nell promised, climbing into the car. "Thanks again."

Jane and Cal stood by the door of the clinic until Nell had pulled out of sight.

"You hungry?" Cal asked, his hand on Jane's shoulder.

"Starving," she confessed.

"Me, too."

They warmed the takeout in the microwave and sat side by side on the examination table, holding the cardboard containers on their laps.

"This tastes like heaven," Jane told him between bites. The enchilada sauce and melting cheese dripped from her plastic fork.

"That's because we're hungry."

"I'm sorry our dinner date was ruined." She did feel bad about that. Cal had been thoughtful and patient—bringing them their meal, comforting Nell, sitting here for hours—and she wanted him to know how much she appreciated it.

"I'm not," he surprised her by saying. Her reaction must have shown in her eyes because he added, "It was good to see you in action. You're a damned good doctor."

His praise flustered her and she looked away. "Thank you."

"You were great with the kid," he said, and hopped down from the table to toss the container in the garbage.

"I appreciated your help. Nell was frazzled and anxious." She crossed the room to discard her leftovers; when she turned around, she inadvertently bumped into Cal.

His arm shot out to balance her, although she wasn't in danger of falling. The move had been instinctive, but the moment he touched her, she froze. Cal did, too. It was a little thing, of no importance, but it caught her off guard. The shaken look on Cal's face told her he was equally affected.

Then before her instincts could warn her, it happened. Cal bent his head and kissed her. It was almost as though that, too, was an accident. The kiss was hard, quick, their mouths moist and warm. Then it was over.

Jane stared at him, unblinking. Cal stared back. They studied each other for a startled moment. He seemed about to apologize when he suddenly grinned, instead. It was one of the sexiest smiles she'd ever seen. Then he kissed her again.

As kisses went, this one was innocent. Simple. Yet Jane trembled with the aftershock. She'd been too long without a man, she decided. That was why this rancher had such a powerful effect on her senses.

Desperate to steer her mind away from what had just happened, she said, "I...I spoke with Dovie Boyd recently. She happened to mention a ghost town."

Cal frowned, but Jane wasn't sure his displeasure was the result of their kiss or her comment. Possibly both.

"Bitter End," Jane added. "Have you ever heard of it?"

He nodded and shoved his hands into his pockets.

He wasn't forthcoming with any more information. "Then there really *is* a ghost town in the area?" she prodded.

Cal shrugged.

Jane made herself busy about the room, putting away her supplies. "Have you been there?"

He didn't answer until she turned to face him, and even then his eyes avoided hers. "Once, as a kid."

Her excitement grew. "Will you take me there? I'd love to see what it's like now."

"Jane, I can't."

His refusal bewildered her. "Why not?"

"I don't even know if I could find it."

"But we could do that together. I'll be taking more riding lessons, and we've got to move me out of the corral at some point. This would give me a goal, some incentive."

"I don't think so."

"Why not?" Jane could tell he wasn't pleased with her persistence.

"It's dangerous there."

"All I want to do is see it," she said, unwilling to give up without an argument. "One time, that's all I'm asking."

"It's not a good idea."

It was his attitude that got to her—as if she were a child who had to settle for *because I said so* as an excuse. How could he kiss her one moment and insult her the next?

"Is there a reason for this?" she asked, her voice growing cool.

"A very good one."

She waited for him to explain himself, and when he didn't, she said it for him. "It's because I'm an outsider, isn't it? Because I wasn't born and raised here. It's all right for me to give three years of my life to this community, but I'll never be fully accepted." The strength of her feelings shocked Jane.

It hurt that he'd categorically deny her the one thing she'd asked.

His features softened. "Jane, that's not it."

"Then what *is* it?"

"First, I don't know where Bitter End is. I really don't. Second, I've got better things to do with my time than wander around the countryside looking for some old town best forgotten."

This was quite a speech for Cal. "But you've already been there once."

"Years ago," he said, "when I was a kid."

"You should be able to find it again."

"Jane, *no.*"

The evening had started out with great promise; now this. What Cal Patterson didn't understand was that she was an old hand at getting what she wanted. She'd been forced to acquire the skills, to refine the tactics. Medical school had taught her that. She'd learned how to deal with older physicians who felt women had no place in medicine. She'd come face-to-face with the old-boy network more than once. People assumed this sort of outdated thinking wasn't prevalent any longer, but they were wrong. She'd seen it and dealt with it on a daily basis, and learned there was more than one way to achieve what she wanted.

"I'm sorry to hear you won't help me find the ghost town," she said softly.

"It's no place for a greenhorn."

"I see." Her tone was noncommittal.

He narrowed his eyes. "Why do I have the feeling I'm butting my head against a brick wall?"

So he knew. "I'll find Bitter End with or without you," she said matter-of-factly.

Cal's eyes closed for an instant. "And if I decide not to continue with the riding lessons, you'll have someone else teach you, too?"

"Yes." She wasn't going to lie about her intentions. That was exactly what she'd do if necessary—only she hoped it wouldn't be. "I'd much rather continue with you, though." She took a deep breath. "Cal, I'm not trying to be manipulative here. But I want to see this town. I'll admit I've become kind of obsessed with it. And I'll do whatever it takes to get there."

It was several moments before he responded. "It's not safe in Bitter End."

"So you said."

"The town's...evil."

"Evil? You mean there are *ghosts*?"

"Not that type of evil." He paced the room, as though it was impossible for him to stand still any longer. "Grady Weston, Glen and I found Bitter End a number of years ago. I must have been about fifteen at the time, high on adventure. Fearless, like all kids that age. Cocky, some might say."

"I wouldn't have thought that was so long ago," she joked.

He didn't crack a smile. "We searched for weeks, the three of us. It was summer and we went out looking every day we could. We studied maps, even checked out an old journal that had belonged to Grady's father and had a few cryptic hints."

"But you found the town," Jane said, her voice rising with excitement.

"Yes, eventually we located it."

"Did you explore? What was it like? I'd love to see it! Oh, Cal, please reconsider."

His sigh was deep and troubled. "You can't imagine how thrilled we were when we stumbled across it. We'd been searching all that time, and then one afternoon there it was. Surprisingly most of the buildings were intact."

"That's incredible!" Just wait until her mother heard this. She'd want to know every detail.

"But it wasn't what we expected," Cal told her, his eyes somber.

"How do you mean?"

"There's something wrong in that town. Like I said, something evil. We all felt it the moment we rode down the street. The horses felt it, too. The entire time we were there, they were skittish."

"Something evil?" This made no sense to Jane. "What exactly was the feeling like?"

"I've thought about it a lot in the last few months, ever since Grady told me Savannah's been out there."

"Savannah Smith?" Jane wondered if Cal realized he'd handed her a way of locating the town.

"She went there looking for old roses. According to what Grady said, she felt it, too. That same feeling."

"Well, what *was* it?"

Cal shook his head. "It's impossible to describe. I've never experienced anything like it before or since."

"Try," she pleaded.

"Like there's a rope tightening around my

chest," he said, struggling to find the words. "A feeling of sadness. Loss. As though more than a century wasn't enough time to wipe out the grief or the agony of whatever happened."

"I'd still like to see it for myself," she told him.

"I figured you would." His tone was resigned.

"Does this mean you'll take me?" She clasped her hands, prayerlike. She didn't want another riding teacher. She liked the one she had. And she wanted Cal to be her guide to Bitter End; if there was danger in the town, she'd rather he was with her.

"All right," he finally agreed. "We'll go look for it."

Overjoyed, Jane threw her arms around his neck and hugged him. The next instant Cal wrapped his arms around her waist and pulled her against him. Without warning, his mouth crashed down on hers. The kiss was urgent. Exciting. Cal didn't give Jane an opportunity to break it off, not that she would have, but gradually, as though he realized what he'd done, he mellowed the kiss. He wove his fingers into her hair, then slowly, cautiously, they began to relax against each other. Jane moved her lips, opening to him—and the excitement built again.

Cal groaned. He twisted his mouth against hers, seeking more, and Jane was all too willing to comply. She wasn't sure a man had ever kissed her quite like this. With such need, such intensity.

When he broke away, they were both gasping. "I...I think I need to sit down," Jane said, reaching for the nearest chair and lowering herself into it.

"Me, too," Cal said.

Involuntarily she raised her hands to her lips. The kiss had been fierce. Wonderful.

"I didn't mean for that to happen," he said next. But instead of sitting, he stalked about the room.

"I know."

"I think you should realize I've already decided it would be...ill-advised for us to get involved."

He sounded so absurdly formal. Had she been in full possession of her wits, she would have challenged him, demanded to know his reasons. But his kisses had left her senseless. Her own pride played a role in her reaction, too. She just looked at him, unwilling, unable, to respond.

"I don't mean to insult you," he added.

"You didn't," she was quick to assure him, then hesitated, more confused than offended. "Are you saying you want to put a halt to the riding lessons?"

"Not at all. When will you be ready again?"

From the intense look in his eyes, Jane had the feeling he was inquiring about a lot more than horseback riding. "Tomorrow?" She raised her eyes to his. She wasn't shy or cowardly or afraid of risks. Medicine wasn't a career for a woman who was weak at heart. If she had been, Jane wouldn't have lasted a month in medical school.

"I'll see you at three," he said on his way out the door.

"I'll be there," she called after him. It'd take more than stubborn pride to upset her. She had a strong feeling that Cal Patterson had met his match—and an even stronger feeling that she'd met hers.

RICHARD WAS BORED but he was smart enough to realize that the moment he left Bitter End, he'd risk being caught and hauled to jail.

By now, despite switching license plates, the truck he'd "borrowed" would be listed in a police computer as stolen.

Relieving his boredom by leaving the ghost town was a risk he couldn't afford to take, although it was damned tempting.

Leaning his chair against the side of the old hotel, he strummed a few chords on his guitar. Only, it wasn't nearly as much fun to play without an audience.

He reached for the half-empty whiskey bottle and indulged in a healthy swig. The liquor wasn't going to last, he could see that. He'd drunk twice as much as he'd estimated. His limited supply would need to see him through the next few months. A bottle wasn't much company on the long lonely nights, but it was all he had. Hell, a man took what he could get.

He strummed a few more chords on the guitar and sang halfheartedly. If his life had taken a different turn, he might have entered show business, made a name for himself. He would've enjoyed that.

He returned the bottle to his lips, shuddering at the potency of the drink. Enough liquor would help him forget. Or help him remember. Problem was, he couldn't decide which he wanted anymore.

He tipped back his head and shouted with everything in him, "Is anyone home?" He waited for a response and was both relieved and disheartened when none came.

Even a ghost might be some company.

According to the days he'd marked off on the calendar, this was Friday night. If he'd still been in Promise, instead of hiding up in this godforsaken ghost town, he'd probably be at Billy D's, drinking with the boys. Shooting the breeze, playing pool or maybe a game of darts.

He'd be singing, too, along with the jukebox. A little David Allan Coe, the ex-con turned singer. His music could get raunchy and off-color, but Richard didn't mind. It was just the thing for a Friday night at the saloon.

But this Friday—and how many others to follow?—Richard would be alone.

What he missed even more was female companionship. He could have had a cozy love nest here had he been thinking clearly. But everything had come down on him and there hadn't been time to find a woman to bring with him—or maybe two.

The loneliness wouldn't be half so bad with a couple of sweet young things to keep him occupied. Yeah, he could've convinced them this was an adventure. And he could've let them fight over him, which was guaranteed to be entertaining. Not too hard on his ego, either. Women didn't walk away when *he* was around. All except Ellie Frasier, now Ellie Patterson. Richard frowned. He didn't know what he'd done wrong. Her choosing Glen Patterson over him hurt his pride.

"She's a fool," he said aloud.

One day Ellie would regret her choice, Richard was sure of it. She could have married him, instead of that hick Patterson. Everything had gone downhill after that.

The creditors had started closing in and it'd become impossible to hide the charges he'd made on Grady's accounts. As soon as Grady learned the truth, he would have kicked him out. But Richard hadn't given his brother the chance; moving with speed, he'd left Promise before any of it came to light.

He'd carefully worked out every detail of his plan, stocking up on stolen food and supplies for weeks beforehand. It wasn't an easy task, but he'd been at his deceptive best. He was proud of the way he'd pulled it off, too, keeping his activities hidden from the family.

Grady and Savannah were pathetic, really.

As far as Richard was concerned, his brother and sister deserved everything they got. Anyone that trusting needed to be taught a lesson. Richard had burned them twice, and it hadn't been difficult. He wondered if they'd ever learn; he suspected they wouldn't. They weren't the type, neither one of them. He experienced a twinge of guilt, but refused to waste time on a useless emotion. Grady and Savannah were nothing short of gullible. He looked at it this way—he'd done them a favor. Taught them a life lesson. He couldn't help it if they were slow learners.

A shooting star blazed across the autumn sky and Richard raised his bottle in salute. He wished he had a woman on his arm, but okay, that wasn't possible. His little home away from home was a damn sight better than a jail cell, and that was where he was headed if the law ever got hold of him.

Life was much too complicated, Richard mused. What had started out as a simple transaction back in New York had gone sour. The bad taste of it lingered in his mouth, but there was no use fretting about it now.

In addition to his many talents, Richard Weston was a survivor. He might be down but he wasn't out, and once his current troubles came to an end, he'd be back on his feet.

If Ellie had married him, he would've used her inheritance to pay off some rather dangerous debts—and to grease the right palms. But she was with Glen. Stupid woman. She didn't know a good thing when she saw it.

He tipped back the bottle, took another drink and immediately felt worse. He was lonely and restless. All the self-talk in the world wasn't going to change that. While he might be safe, he wasn't happy.

Chapter Six

Jane removed the blood-pressure cuff from Ruth Bishop's upper arm and noted the reading on her chart. Ruth's diastolic and systolic numbers were well within the normal range, which was good. The medication was doing its job.

"Overall, how are you feeling?" Jane asked as she reached for her prescription pad to write a renewal.

"Good," Ruth said, after a short hesitation.

Jane looked up. "Is there anything else you'd like me to check? You're here now and I'd hate to have you think of something later." Jane held office hours on Saturday morning because it seemed a convenient time for a lot of people. If Ruth decided, once she got home, that she *did* have some other concern, Jane wouldn't be available again until Monday. Not only that, Ruth would have to make the long drive a second time.

Jane waited quietly for a minute or so.

Ruth finally spoke. "Actually it's my daughter-in-law," she said.

Jane sat down and made herself comfortable. It'd

taken her a while to realize that, when it came to confidences, people shared at their own pace and in their own way. Not just the people in Promise, Texas, but people everywhere.

"Nell was in last night with Jeremy," Jane said, wanting Ruth to know she was familiar with her daughter-in-law.

"I know. Jeremy said that for a lady doctor you weren't half-bad."

Jane unsuccessfully hid a smile.

"He meant that as a compliment," Ruth said, her cheeks growing pink.

"Don't worry, Ruth, I hear that all the time."

"It's difficult for some folks to get used to the idea of a female doctor."

Ruth wasn't telling Jane something she didn't already know.

"I'm living with Nell," Ruth explained, "helping her out when I can. Encouraging her. It was a blow to both of us when Jake died… I never expected my son would join his father before me." Her eyes teared up, and Jane leaned forward to hand her a tissue. Ruth thanked her in a choked voice and dabbed her eyes.

"So…what about Nell?" Jane asked gently, giving the older woman time to compose herself.

"Early this morning I found her in the living room weeping. That's not like her. She's not a woman who shows her pain. When we buried Jake, it was Nell who remained strong, who comforted the family, who held us all together. I don't know what we would've done without her."

From her psychology classes, Jane remembered

that in a family crisis there was usually one member who remained emotionally steady for others to lean on for support. She'd seen the truth of this time and again. Sometimes family members traded roles, almost taking turns, at comforting and helping one another through a crisis.

"Nell shed her share of tears, I know that," Ruth said, "but she did it privately. She loved my son, grieves for him still."

"I'm sure that's true," Jane said. She hardly knew Nell, but the widow was unmistakably a strong independent woman, someone she'd like to call a friend.

"Jeremy's broken arm shook her more than I realized. I wasn't home at the time. The Moorhouse sisters, Betty Knoll and I play bridge on Friday nights. Edwina and Lily bring out their cordial— same recipe Dovie uses—and we let down our hair and relax."

Jane could picture the four older women and suspected they were crackerjack bridge players.

"Nell told me Jeremy had climbed on the tractor. That he fell off and broke his arm." Ruth grew quiet for a moment. "You may not know this, but Jake died in a tractor accident. It must have been terribly upsetting for Nell finding Jeremy by the tractor. Especially since she's the one who found Jake. He was still alive and in shock, but was gone before help could reach him."

"I'm so sorry," Jane murmured. She could only imagine the horror of finding your husband trapped beneath a tractor. Nell had been pale and shaken when she arrived with Jeremy, Jane remembered;

she must have been reliving that unbearable time. Thank heaven Cal had been at the clinic and was able to distract Nell while she dealt with the injured boy.

"It's been almost three years since Jake's been gone. It doesn't seem like it could be that long, but it is."

"It's a big adjustment, losing a son." Jane said softly.

"And losing a husband. Last night I found Nell sitting in her rocker by the fireplace," Ruth said, continuing with her story. "It was three in the morning, and when I asked her what woke her up, Nell told me she hadn't been to bed yet."

"Had she been up with Jeremy?" The question was prompted by Jane's concern that perhaps the pain medication hadn't worked adequately. After the shock of a broken bone, Jeremy needed his rest. His mother did, too.

"No. Nell was...remembering." Ruth fell silent for a moment. "I...I worry about my daughter-in-law," she admitted. "It's time she moved on with her life. Met someone else."

Jane said nothing, preferring to let the other woman speak.

"I don't think it's a good idea for her to spend the rest of her life grieving for Jake," Ruth said, her own voice trembling with emotion. "I know...knew my son and he wouldn't have wanted that."

"Have you told her this?" Jane asked.

"Oh, yes, a number of times. She brushes it off. Last summer, for the Cattlemen's Association dance, she received two invitations. I was ecstatic, thinking it was past time the men in this town paid her some attention.''

Jane was thinking Nell had done better than she had herself. No one had asked her, but then, she'd been new to the community and hadn't met a lot of people yet. By that she meant Cal. He would've been her first choice had she known him.

''Nell turned down both offers,'' Ruth said, pinching her lips in disapproval. ''No amount of coaxing could get her to change her mind, either.'' She exhaled noisily and Jane recognized Ruth's impatience with her daughter-in-law. ''As it turned out, Emma had an upset tummy that night, so Nell made a quick appearance at the dance but came home within the hour. I was baby-sitting and I told her to stay as long as she wanted—have a good time, I said, but she'd have none of it.''

It sounded to Jane as though Emma's upset stomach had been a convenient excuse for Nell to hurry home.

''How can I encourage her?'' Ruth asked.

This was at the heart of her worries, Jane realized. ''You can't,'' she said.

''But it's been almost three years,'' Ruth said again.

''Nell has to be the one to recognize when it's time. No one else can do that for her.''

''I know, but I'd like her to get out more. Socialize. Spend time with her friends, but she hardly even does that. Nell works too hard and laughs too little.''

''It's not something you can force,'' Jane said. ''Nell will know when she's ready.''

"I hope it's soon," Ruth murmured. "My son was a wonderful man, but she's too fine a woman to pine for him the rest of her life. Much too fine."

Jane was sure that was true.

STORM CLOUDS darkened the afternoon. Glancing toward the sky, Cal hurried outside. Electrical storms weren't uncommon in the Texas hill country, and he wanted his livestock in the shelter of the barn.

The dogs helped him and he'd gotten Atta Girl and a chestnut mare named Cheyenne safely into the barn when he saw Jane's car pull into the yard. Damn, with the approach of the storm, he'd forgotten about the lesson. Despite that, she hadn't been far from his thoughts all day. Not since the moment he'd first kissed her.

He didn't know what had driven him to do anything so foolish, especially after insisting there was no future in this relationship. Impulse, he supposed—an impulse he planned to avoid from now on.

Frightened by the thunder, Moonshine, Glen's favorite gelding, pranced about the yard, making him difficult to catch. He wouldn't have given Glen nearly as much trouble, but there was nothing Cal could do about that now.

The wind howled and the first fat drops of rain fell haphazardly from the sky. "Can I help?" Jane had to shout to be heard.

"Go in the house before you get soaked," Cal ordered. The rain was falling steadily now, and Cal knew it would only grow more intense.

"I can do something!"

He should've known she'd insist on helping him. Dr. Texas wasn't the type who took orders willingly. Cal groaned; he certainly knew how to pick 'em. He couldn't be attracted to a docile eager-to-please female. Oh no, that would be too easy. Instead, he had to go and complicate his life with a woman whose personality was as strong and obstinate as his own.

Against his wishes, Jane ran to the corral and stood on the opposite side, waving her hands high above her head. To Cal's amazement Moonshine had a change of heart. Either that, or the quarter horse was so unsettled by the sight of a California girl flapping her arms around, he figured the barn was the safest place for him. In an abrupt turn-around, the gelding trotted obediently into the barn, one of the dogs barking at his heels.

Cal followed him inside and out of the rain. He waited for Jane to join him before closing the door. The rain fell in earnest, a real downpour, pounding the ground with such force the drops ricocheted three inches upward.

Cal led Moonshine into his stall. "I didn't think you'd come, what with the storm and all," he told Jane.

"I wasn't sure I should."

It went against his pride to let her know how pleased he was she had.

"Do you want me to drive home?" she asked, sounding oddly uncertain and a bit defensive.

It was the way he'd feel had circumstances been reversed. "You're here now. The weather's a write-off but we'll make the best of it." Which shouldn't be too hard. Dr. Texas looked damn good in her hip-hugging jeans and boots.

He removed his jacket and handed it to her. "Let's make a run for the house." Opening the barn door, he looked out and cringed. The rain was still coming down in torrents and it was almost impossible to see across the yard. They'd be drenched to the skin by the time they reached the house.

Holding the jacket above her head for protection, Jane moved beside him to view the downpour. "My goodness, does it rain like this often?"

"Often enough," he muttered.

"I've never seen anything like it."

Seeing she'd been born and raised in Southern California, Cal could believe that. He'd read about small towns near Death Valley where the children had never seen rain at all.

"You ready?" he asked.

"Any time," she said, with a game smile.

Lightning flashed. Not willing to wait any longer, Cal offered Jane his hand. She clasped it tightly and held the jacket over her head with her free hand. They sprinted toward the house, sliding a bit on the muddy ground. He kept his pace deliberately even, fearing she might slip.

Breathing hard, they burst into the house together. Jane released Cal's hand immediately. The water dripped from him as if he'd just stepped out of the shower, and his clothes were plastered to his skin.

"You're drenched," Jane said, and gave him back his jacket. Despite the protection it had provided, her hair and face glistened with rainwater.

"So are you," he said, and for the life of him, he couldn't pull his gaze away from hers.

"Not like you." She moistened her lips with her tongue and that was Cal's downfall. He'd already promised himself there wouldn't be a repeat of the kiss they'd shared last night, but nothing could have stopped him from sampling her lips once more. He leaned forward and pressed his mouth to hers.

He wasn't sure what he expected, but not her sigh of welcome. Nor had he anticipated her stepping farther into his embrace. His breathing grew heavy and so did hers. The kiss deepened and she slipped her arms around his neck and moved even closer. The feel of her soft body against his was enough to make him weak at the knees.

He lifted his head. "I'm getting you all wet."

"I know."

"You shouldn't have come," he whispered, although his head and his heart waged battle.

"Do you want me to leave?"

"No." His response was instantaneous. Direct. Reluctantly he eased her out of his arms. "I'll go change."

"I'll put on a pot of coffee."

He nodded and headed toward the stairway, taking the steps two at a time. Every minute not spent with her felt wasted, and he was a frugal man.

He stripped off his shirt, then flung it aside, drying himself with a towel. He reached for a sweater and pulled it over his head. He'd just donned a clean pair of jeans and had stepped back into his boots when the electric lights flickered and went off.

The house was almost completely dark. Even

though it was midafternoon, the heavy black clouds closed out the light.

"Jane," he shouted from the top of the stairs, "are you okay?"

"I'm fine," she called back.

"I'll be right there." Cal draped his wet clothes over the edge of the bathtub and ran a comb through his hair before going downstairs. He got a flashlight from the hallway and found Jane in the kitchen standing next to the stove.

"I guess we'll have to do without the coffee," she said.

"Will wine do?" he asked.

"Great idea." His eyes were adjusting to the darkness and he saw her smile at him.

It would be easy to get lost in one of those smiles. "I'll get a fire going." He took her hand and led her into the living room. He knelt in front of the brick fireplace, arranged the kindling, then placed a couple of logs on top. The match flared briefly and ignited the wood. Soon a fire burned invitingly, its warmth spreading into the room.

"This is cozy, isn't it?" Jane said, huddling close to the fire.

"I'll be back in a minute with the wine." As it happened, he had a number of bottles left over from the wedding that had never taken place. He'd wanted Glen and Ellie to use the wine at theirs, but Glen had declined, insisting Cal save it for a rainy day. Like right now, Cal thought wryly.

He returned with a corkscrew, two goblets and a bottle of merlot.

He sat on the carpet with Jane, his back supported

by the sofa, a glass of wine in his hand. Jane sat next to him, chin resting on her bent knees.

"I'm glad you're here," he said, not looking at her. It was a big admission, seeing as he'd told her— twice—she shouldn't have come.

"I'm glad I'm here, too."

He put his arm around her shoulders and she scooted closer to his side. She turned to him with another one of her potent smiles. It was an invitation to kiss her again, an invitation he wasn't about to ignore.

She wanted his kisses, her smile said. Cal had thought of little else from the moment they sat down in front of the fire. He'd attempted to discipline his response to her, but his resolve weakened by the moment, and he'd all but given up.

He lowered his head and watched as her eyes closed. He could deny himself no longer. The kiss that followed was intense and passionate. He hadn't meant it to be—but he couldn't help it, either. His mouth played on hers until he groaned.

Thunder exploded, and for an instant Cal thought it was the beat of his own heart. Jane had that kind of effect on him. He broke off the kiss and, closing his eyes, leaned his head back against the sofa. Drawing in several deep breaths, he struggled to find his equilibrium.

He couldn't make himself stop wanting her. But it wasn't right; he knew that. This relationship had no future.

At last he straightened and took a sip of his wine. Jane did, too, and he noticed that her hand trembled slightly. His was shaking, too.

He'd rarely been more unnerved. He thought of telling her about Jennifer, then changed his mind, afraid she'd read something more into the information than he intended. And yet he couldn't say what his intentions were.

"Are you cold?" he asked, diverting his attention from these dangerous thoughts.

"No. How about you?"

The wine had warmed him. The wine and her kisses. "I'm fine."

All of a sudden, they were shy with each other.

Probably in an effort to distract herself, Jane started a conversation, mentioning people in town she was beginning to know. Cal eagerly joined in, answering her questions, bringing up other names. At least when they were talking, he wasn't thinking about making love to her.

The hell he wasn't!

"This has got to stop," he said, and at her look of surprise, realized he'd spoken aloud.

"What's got to stop?" Jane asked.

Embarrassed, he couldn't think of a single response. "This," he said, setting his wineglass aside. The next moment she was in his arms again. The kiss started in hunger and progressed to greed. Her response was immediate and she went soft and pliable in his arms.

"Cal?" she whispered, gazing up at him.

"Mm?" He spread a row of moist kisses on her neck and jaw. She moaned softly and rolled her head to one side. His senses filled with the taste of her, the citrusy scent of her. He couldn't make himself quit, couldn't make himself *want* to quit.

She moaned again when he let his tongue slide along the hollow of her throat.

"You wanted something," he reminded her.

"Yes..."

"What?" He worked his way back to her lips.

He wasn't sure how it happened, but soon her head rested on his lap and he was bent over her.

"You're right—we should stop," she murmured with little conviction.

"I couldn't agree with you more," he said, and kissed her again.

She looped her arms around his neck and raised her head from his lap. They strained against each other, trying to get closer, closer. His thoughts—all the reasons kissing Jane wasn't a good idea—didn't mean a thing.

Jane's mouth parted for him and his tongue curled around hers. The next thing he knew, his hand had worked open the front of her blouse and slipped inside to cup a satin-sheathed breast. Her skin was warm to the touch.

This attraction was becoming increasingly dangerous. And harder to resist.

"What should we do?" he asked, needing her to say or do something to stop this.

"I...don't know."

He kissed her again, slowly, thoroughly. "You're a Valley girl."

"No, I'm not! Anyway, you're a rebel."

"You belong in California."

"You punch cattle for a living."

"There's no future in this."

"None whatsoever."

Cal frowned. "Then why do I feel like this?"

"When you know the answer, tell me."

To his dying day Cal wouldn't know what it was about this stubborn beautiful woman that made him laugh the way he did. He threw back his head and howled.

Jane apparently didn't find it all that amusing. She sat upright, then shocked him by climbing over him and straddling his lap. His eyes grew wide with surprise.

His amusement faded when she threw her arms around his neck and teased him with nibbling kisses that left him hungering for more.

"You taking me to find that ghost town, Rebel?" she whispered.

"Do I have a choice?"

"None whatsoever."

He muttered under his breath. "I'll do it, but I won't like it."

She grinned. "There'll be compensations," she promised.

"I'm counting on that."

And then she really kissed him. By the time she finished, he would have gladly taken her anywhere she asked.

FRANK FELT like a schoolboy as he splashed aftershave on his face and studied his reflection in the bathroom mirror. For the first time in eleven years he had a date with someone other than Dovie. He'd rather be with her, but they remained at an impasse and he was tired of fighting a losing battle.

It'd taken him three days to compile a list of candidates and then pare it down to one woman. His decision made, he'd phoned Tammy Lee Kollenborn and invited her to dinner and a movie. It helped soothe his wounded ego when she eagerly accepted.

Of all the eligible women in town, Tammy Lee was the most attractive. She was a fiftyish divorcée who wore a little too much makeup and was friends with Louise Powell; that was the downside. On the other hand, since Louise was the town gossip, word of his seeing Tammy Lee was sure to get back to Dovie.

Tammy Lee had been divorced for twenty years or more, Frank knew, and that was a factor in her favor. She'd dated a number of men in town and revealed no sign of wanting to remarry. Another plus. From what he heard, she received hefty alimony payments. She routinely traveled and had spent one summer in Europe, returning to Promise with some mighty interesting souvenirs. Apparently she'd brought back a giant round mirror festooned with romping nymphs and satyrs. Rumor had it she'd fastened it to the ceiling above her bed. In time, Frank might have the opportunity to investigate that particular piece of gossip for himself.

Frank didn't know Tammy Lee well, but she was exactly the type of date he was looking for. Once Dovie heard about this, she was sure to have a change of heart. If she didn't, well, that was that. He'd done everything within his power to get her to see reason. Short of marrying her, which he refused to do.

He reached for his jacket and headed out the front door, grateful the rain had ceased. He was starting slow, easing into this relationship. Dinner, followed by a movie. They could chat over the meal, get comfortable with each other. A movie was a good way to end the evening, no pressure to carry on a conversation.

Frank picked up Tammy Lee at her house. She opened the door and beamed him a broad smile. "I can't tell you how pleased I was when you phoned," she said, draping a fringed wrap over her shoulders. "The first person I called was Louise."

Louise Powell. Well, it was no less than he'd expected. Louise might be a blabbermouth, but this time, it was to his advantage.

"You look terrific," he said, thinking a compliment early in the evening would put them on a good footing. She wore a gold lamé jumpsuit with a jeweled belt that emphasized her trim waist and hips. He especially appreciated her high heels, found them sexy. Fewer and fewer women wore them these days.

Tammy Lee stopped and checked her reflection in the hallway mirror, then smiled. "What a nice thing to say."

Frank waited for her to return the compliment, but she didn't. He led her outside and opened the car door, wanting to impress her with his manners. Dovie had always enjoyed the little things he did to show her he cared.

"I'm a modern woman," Tammy Lee said after he'd climbed into the car and started the engine. "I can get my own door, but it's real sweet of you to do that."

"You don't want me to open your car door?"

"It isn't necessary, Frank."

He smiled and decided he was pleased. This was a woman who spoke her mind, who asked for what she wanted. He respected that.

They chose to eat at the Chili Pepper, and their appearance created something of a stir. Frank felt he should apologize for the attention they received.

"Don't worry about it," she said, graciously dismissing his concern. "I know what it's like when a longtime relationship ends. People are curious, wanting to know the details."

People like Louise Powell, Frank added silently.

Frank ordered a steak and a baked potato with all the fixings. He'd lost a few pounds pining for Dovie, and was ready to make up for lost time.

He was mildly disappointed when Tammy Lee asked for a plain green salad with red-wine vinegar.

"I'm watching my weight," she explained.

Frank guessed that her trim figure demanded sacrifice. He ordered a cold beer to go with his meal, while Tammy Lee ordered a highball, her first of three. He wondered about the calories in those, but didn't ask. At four-fifty a drink, she could have ordered the steak. She surprised him further when she asked to see the dessert menu.

"Every once in a while I allow myself a goodie," she said.

Frank never ate restaurant desserts. Dovie, when he could convince her to go out, refused to let him eat a pie baked in an aluminum-foil tin. She insisted she could outbake anything that came from a freezer. He'd never argued with her.

Tammy Lee ordered apple pie à la mode.

"Save room for popcorn," he told her.

She shook her head. "I don't touch the stuff."

"Oh," he said. That was his favorite part of going to the movies. Yes, the theater charged outrageous prices, but it was a rare treat and one of the few indulgences Dovie enjoyed, too. They bought the largest bag, with butter, and shared it.

"I was sorry to hear about your breakup with Dovie," Tammy Lee said, sounding anything but.

"Yes, well, these things happen." Frank wasn't willing to discuss Dovie with another woman.

"I've always liked her," Tammy Lee said.

That statement was patently insincere.

"She's a special lady," Frank said, growing uncomfortable with this conversation.

Tammy Lee frowned slightly. "I did understand you correctly, didn't I? You and Dovie are no longer seeing each other?"

Frank shifted in his seat. "Do you mind if we change the subject?" he asked pointedly.

"Of course not. It's just that, well, I know you and Dovie were...close, if you catch my drift."

Frank wasn't sure he did. "How do you mean?"

"Well..." Tammy Lee lowered her voice significantly. "I understand you spent the night with Dovie at least twice a week."

Frank opened his mouth to tell her it wasn't any of her damn business how close he and Dovie were, but she stopped him.

"The only reason I mention this, Frank, is that..." She paused and sent him a pained look. "This is rather embarrassing, and I do hope you'll forgive me for being blunt, but I'm in a position to help you through these difficult times.''

"Difficult times?" What was she talking about?

"Physically," she whispered, beaming him another one of her smiles. "I'm currently without a man in my life and I'd welcome your attentions, Sheriff Hennessey."

He didn't think a woman had ever shocked him more. Frank shook his head in wonderment. Two years. It'd taken him two full years of courting Dovie before she'd allowed him into her bed. And even after all the time they'd been involved, she was uncomfortable making love without the sanction of marriage. Yet this woman was brazenly letting him know she'd welcome him to her bed on their first date. Sure, he'd admit to a mild fantasy about her supposed sensual bedroom—but checking it out on their first date? What in hell had happened to the world since he'd been out of circulation?

"Well?" Tammy Lee asked.

"Perhaps we should discuss this at a later time," Frank said.

"Have I shocked you, Frank?" she asked, then laughed coyly.

"Shocked me? What makes you ask that?"

"Your ears have gone all red." She snickered as if she found this highly humorous.

Tammy Lee's words irritated him, but he attempted to disguise his reaction. Frank was actually looking forward to the movie for the simple reason that they wouldn't be speaking. She said the most outrageous things, and he was getting tired of it.

The theater in Promise had only one screen. The

seats were rather worn, but comfortable. The feature films weren't always first-run, but since it was the only show in town, few complained.

Frank purchased their tickets and was putting his change back into his wallet when Tammy Lee decided to get possessive. She rubbed his back affectionately and cozied up to his side, wrapping her hands around his upper arm. He shouldn't be surprised, he supposed; her actions were certainly in keeping with her conversation.

When he looked up, he saw the reason his date had started to cling to him like a blackberry vine. Standing only a few feet away from him was Dovie Boyd, holding a small bag of popcorn and a paper cup of soda. Her eyes widened with a flash of shock and pain. He feared she was about to drop her drink and admired her for her fast recovery.

Tammy Lee all but draped her arms around his neck, nuzzling his ear like some annoying insect he longed to bat away.

Dovie offered them both a brave if shaky smile. "Hello, Frank. Hello, Tammy Lee," she said. And then, with the grace of the lady she was, she turned and walked into the theater.

Chapter Seven

Jane saw Cal every day after their rainy afternoon. The riding lessons continued, but they found other reasons to be together, too. After their first date he no longer made an issue of their not becoming involved and she was glad. She particularly liked meeting him at the ranch, liked seeing him in his own world, which was new and strange and enchanting to her.

It was Sunday, two weeks after the storm. For her riding lesson that afternoon, they rode to the farthest pasture with Digger, Cal's dog, racing along beside them. The day was glorious, a perfect autumn day with temperatures still in the mid-seventies.

Jane had become almost comfortable in the saddle. Either she'd built up calluses on that part of her anatomy, she thought wryly, or she'd gained skill. Probably a combination of both.

Jane frequently mentioned Cal in her letters and phone calls home. She'd taken a great deal of ribbing from her father about this penchant she had for horseback riding. He told her he'd thought she'd outgrown it when she was thirteen. Like many girls, she'd been horse-crazy, reading horse stories and collecting figurines. In a way, what Cal had given her was the opportunity to live a long-ago dream.

"You're quiet this afternoon," Cal remarked when they reached the crest of the hill.

The view of the pasture below was breathtaking. Cattle grazed there, scattered picturesquely about the fields. Cal had explained earlier that most of his herd had been sold off now, and he was wintering a relatively small number of bulls and heifers.

"I'm thinking," she said, in response to his observation.

"I hope it isn't taxing you too much."

"The only thing that taxes me is you."

"Me?" He pretended to be insulted.

"You keep putting me off."

The laughter faded from his eyes. He knew exactly what she was talking about. She hated to be a pest, but she wasn't going to let him delay much longer. The ghost town beckoned her; she'd actually started to dream about it. Her mother had mailed her a thick book about Texas ghost towns, but Bitter End wasn't included. It amazed her that an entire town could be tucked away in these hills and so few people knew about it.

"I spoke with Grady and Savannah this afternoon," Cal told her.

"Why didn't you say something sooner?" she asked. It was what she'd been waiting to hear, as Cal knew very well. Savannah had been to the town earlier in the year and apparently found the most incredible old roses blooming in the cemetery. Having visited the town fairly recently, Savannah would be able to give her and Cal directions and save them the trouble of a long search.

When Cal didn't answer, she pressed, "Aren't you going to tell me what they said?"

"In a little while."

Jane was beginning to understand Cal. He didn't like being pressured and would eventually get to the point—but he preferred to do it without coaxing from her. Her patience was usually rewarded, and considering how good he'd been to her, how generous with his time, she could wait.

"This truly is God's country, isn't it?" she said. Cal had helped her develop a love of the land. He didn't preach or lecture about it. Instead, he allowed her to see and feel it for herself. He'd taught her to appreciate what it meant to be a real cowboy, too. Some people thought that cowboys were a dying breed, but for Cal, the work and the life were vital and worthwhile. There wasn't a task on the Lonesome Coyote Ranch he couldn't handle—branding cattle to breaking horses to birthing calves.

"Do you mean that, about this being God's country?" he asked.

"Yes." And she did. The land was astonishingly beautiful. What she'd come to love about it was what Cal referred to as "elbow room." The hill country was gentle rolling hills, and pastureland that was fresh, green, limitless.

Cal had told her he could ride as far as the eye could see, to the horizon and beyond, and not meet another soul. This was something she was only beginning to fathom. So much space!

"What about California?" he asked.

"It's beautiful, too, but not like this."

Cal shook his head. "Too populated. That stuff about earthquakes—it seems to me Mother Nature's saying there're just too many people living in one spot and she's just trying to shake them loose."

He glanced her way as if expecting her to argue with him. She merely smiled and shrugged. She had no intention of ruining a perfect afternoon by getting involved in some pointless argument. Not when the wind was gently blowing in her face and the sweet smells of earth and grass rose up to meet her.

The silence out here took time to accept. At first she'd felt the need to fill their rides with chatter, but as she spent more and more time around Cal, she'd begun to appreciate the lack of sound, to stop fearing it. Cal, by his own admission, wasn't much of a talker. He'd shown her that silence had its own sound, but with the frantic pace of her life, she'd been unable to hear it.

They dismounted, and the two horses drank from the creek. Jane walked over to an oak and leaned against the trunk, one leg bent. Cal picked a handful of wildflowers and handed her the small bouquet.

She rewarded him with a kiss on his cheek. From the way his eyes flared she knew he would've liked to kiss her properly. They'd done plenty of that lately, their attraction growing each time they met. Cal backed away from her now, as if that would help remove him from temptation.

"Tell me what it means to be a rancher," she said.

His gaze held hers. "In what way?"

"I want to know about cattle."

He frowned, then squatted down and plucked a blade of grass. "A good cowboy can tell just by looking at a cow if she's healthy. Her coat'll tell him if she's eating right. The eyes let him know if she's in any kind of trouble."

Jane gave him an encouraging nod. "Go on."

"It's gotten to the point where I can look at a heifer and know when she's ready to spill her first calf," Cal continued. "And one glance at a calf'll tell me if it's suckled that day or been separated from its mother."

Jane was fascinated. "Tell me more."

"It's said some folks don't forget a face. A good rancher doesn't forget a cow."

"You're joking, right?"

His smile told her he wasn't. "They have their own personalities, and they're as individual as you and me. I know that the old cow with the missing horn likes to hide in the willow trees, and the one with a patch of white on its backside is a leader. That one with a cut ear—" he pointed "—is likely to charge a horse and rider.

"My job, if that's what you're asking, is to care for the cows. The cows then tend the calves, and trust me, each cow knows her own calf. She can pick out her baby in a herd of hundreds."

Jane was amazed, but didn't doubt him for a second.

"Cows are constantly on my mind," he said, then cast her a look and added, "or used to be."

She felt a warm glow and smiled.

"I think about them morning, noon and night,"

he went on. "I watch them, study them, and work hard to improve the quality of the herd."

"How do you do that?"

"Every year is a gamble. Weather, disease, the price of beef. With so many things that can go wrong, I cut my losses early and often. If a heifer doesn't breed, she's sold, or if she calves late, she might not get a second chance. I expect a cow to deliver nine calves in nine years, and if she skips a year, I sell her. That might sound harsh, and I often agonize over these decisions. My cattle are more than a commodity to me. The future of Lonesome Coyote is based on the everyday decisions Glen and I make."

Jane had no idea ranching was so complicated. It was a consuming life that required not only hard physical work but research, complex decision-making and business skills.

"Glen and I, along with Grady, have been doing quite a bit of cross-breeding in the past few years, mostly with longhorns. Breeding exceptional cattle isn't as easy as it sounds. Despite the use of artificial insemination and genetics, it's an inexact science that relies on good stock, good weather and good luck." He grinned. "Hey, stop me if I'm lecturing. This is more talking than I normally do in a month."

Jane grinned back. "I hadn't realized there were so many breeds of cattle—although I guess I associate longhorns with Texas."

"At one time there were more than six million longhorns in Texas, but by the late 1920s, they were close to extinction."

"I read that they were making a comeback."

Cal nodded. "They are." He described his cross-breeding program in some detail, and Jane found herself listening avidly to every word. Biology had—naturally—always interested her.

"Cal, I've really enjoyed hearing all this."

His eyes narrowed as if he wasn't sure he should believe her.

"I'm coming to love Texas," she said happily. And Cal Patterson too, but she kept those feelings buried for now, fearing what would happen if she acknowledged how she felt.

"What about California?"

"It's my home—I love it, too."

"You'll go back," he said, his face tightening.

It seemed as if he was challenging her to deny it. Jane didn't, but every day California seemed farther and farther away. Her life was here in Texas now. After years of planning to go into partnership with her uncle Ken, she found the thought starting to lose its appeal. Promise needed her, and she was only beginning to understand why she needed Promise.

"It's time we headed back," Cal said, and went to collect the horses.

"What did Grady and Savannah say about Bitter End?" she blurted, anxious to know.

Cal stopped. "They both tried to talk me out of taking you there."

"Did they succeed?"

He took a long time to answer. "I know you. You're determined to find that town with or without me. You told me as much. And after what they said, I'm inclined to let you try."

"You will take me there, won't you, Cal?" she asked, nervous about his response.

He nodded. "When's your next day off?"

"Wednesday."

"We'll go then."

"Thank you. Oh, thank you!" She raced toward him, threw her arms around his neck and kissed him.

He groaned. "I swear you're going to be the death of me," he muttered.

"But I promise it'll be a great way to die."

THE ACHE INSIDE DOVIE refused to go away. When she hadn't seen or heard from Frank in several days, she'd been almost glad. Every time he came to visit her, it was more and more difficult to send him away. She was afraid that her resolve was weakening. She missed him, missed their times together and the companionship they'd shared. She'd never felt more alone, not even after Marvin had died.

Despite his talk, the last thing she expected Frank to do was go out with another woman, especially this soon. It told her everything she needed to know. Seeing him with Tammy Lee had been one of the most disheartening experiences of her life.

Dovie hated to think unkindly about anyone, but Tammy Lee and Louise Powell were enough to try the patience of a saint. From the way Tammy Lee was clinging to Frank, massaging his back, rubbing her leg down his calf, Dovie realized they'd already become lovers. The thought cut with the sharpness of a knife, and she braced herself against the pain.

The fact that business was slow was a blessing in disguise. In her current state of mind, Dovie was practically useless. She wandered around her shop, unable to sit still, unable to think clearly. Her eyes would start to water for no reason, and somehow it always surprised her; she thought she'd cried all the tears left inside her.

Frank was out of her life once and for all.

The bell above the shop door tinkled and Louise Powell casually strolled in wearing a smug look.

Dovie groaned inwardly. "Hello, Louise," she said, determined to reveal none of her feelings.

"Oh, hello, Dovie." The woman bestowed a saccharine-sweet smile on her.

"Is there anything I can help you find?" she asked, silently praying that whatever Louise wanted was out of stock so she'd leave.

"I'm just browsing," Louise said, wandering from one display to another. She picked up a pair of Kirk's Folly earrings and held them to her face, examining her reflection in the mirror. "Nice," she said, then glanced at the price, raised a brow and set them back down.

"I don't suppose you have any of those rubber piles of dog do-do? They make the funniest practical jokes."

"I'm afraid not," Dovie said. As if she'd actually sell such an outrageous item!

"Hmm," Louise murmured. "So how are you doing these days, Dovie?"

"Wonderful." Dovie gritted her teeth.

"I understand you're leaving on your cruise soon?"

Dovie was looking forward to it more every day. "Yes."

"It must be coming up next week."

Dovie wondered how Louise knew this. "That's right."

"With Frank out of your life, I imagine you're hoping to meet another man."

Dovie said nothing.

"It's a shame, really," Louise said. "I always thought you and Frank made a handsome couple."

Again Dovie said nothing.

"But your loss appears to be Tammy Lee's gain."

Dovie's nails bit into her palms. "I wish them both well," she said.

Louise shook her head. "You're a marvel, Dovie, a real marvel. I don't know if I could be nearly as magnanimous. Tammy Lee was afraid you were offended about her going out with Frank, but I can see that isn't so. You're the picture of generosity."

Dovie forced a smile and hoped Louise didn't notice how brittle it was.

"Tammy Lee's without a man right now," Louise rambled on, "and she's thrilled to be dating Frank. He's such an attractive man."

"Yes, he is." Dovie eased her way toward the front door. Fortunately Louise followed.

"It was good seeing you again," Louise said.

"You, too," Dovie lied.

Louise left and Dovie sank into a chair. The knot was back in the pit of her stomach, and she wondered if it'd ever go away.

That evening Dovie fixed herself a salad but had no appetite. Her home, after thirty years in the same place, suddenly felt too large. Perhaps this was a sign she was ready for a change, a drastic one. She'd been born and raised in Promise, and she'd seen precious little of the world. The upcoming cruise would give her a sample of what life was like outside the great state of Texas, but the cruise was only a few days long. Afterward she'd be back dealing with people like Louise, who relished rubbing Frank's new relationship in her face.

Dovie didn't know if she could bear it. For the first time in her life she seriously considered moving. With the money from the sale of her home and business, plus what was left of Marvin's life insurance, she could live comfortably. Nothing else held her in Promise. She'd stay in touch with the friends she had and make new ones.

The phone rang. Absently Dovie reached for it, studying her home with fresh eyes, wondering how long it would take to sell.

"Hello, Dovie."

The shock of hearing Frank's voice was nearly her undoing. She grabbed hold of the kitchen chair, feeling as though she might faint.

"Frank."

The telephone line hummed with silence.

"How are you?" Frank asked tentatively, as if he didn't know what to say.

She was at a loss about how to respond and decided on a lie, doubting he wanted the truth. "Good, and you?"

"All right. Mostly I was phoning to see if you needed anything."

A new heart to replace the one you stabbed, she

answered silently. "I...don't need anything," she said. "Thank you for asking."

Frank said nothing for a moment. "About the other night...I thought I should explain."

"Frank," she said swiftly, "please, there's no need to explain anything to me."

"But I thought—"

"No, please. I prefer not to know."

"But, Dovie—"

"Whom you date is none of my business. I knew when we parted—when we decided we were at an impasse—that you'd be seeking...companionship elsewhere." Only, she'd credited him with more taste.

"You're the one taking the cruise," he reminded her, the coolness in his voice testifying to his displeasure.

Dovie had nothing to say about her vacation plans, especially not to Frank.

"I've heard about those cruises," Frank continued. "I've seen reruns of 'Love Boat.' People book those fancy liners looking for romance."

"I'm sure that's true in some cases." Not in hers, however. Now seemed as good a time as any to put his mind to rest regarding the future. "I've been giving some thought to...to making certain changes in my life."

"I'm hoping you're about to tell me you want me back." His eagerness was certainly a balm to her wounded pride.

"No, Frank."

"You're going to be looking for another man, right?" he accused.

"No, Frank," she repeated. "I'm not seeking out a new romantic interest." *Unlike you*—but she refused to say it. "I'm thinking of selling the house and moving."

Her words were met with silence, then, "You don't mean it!"

"Yes, Frank, I do."

"But why?"

"You have to admit it's very awkward for us both. You're dating again now and—"

"One date, Dovie. I swear to you that's all it was."

"It doesn't matter."

"I don't even like Tammy Lee."

But there were bound to be others. Dovie didn't know if she had the strength to stand back and smile while the man she loved became involved with another woman. The only thing worse than seeing Frank with someone like Tammy Lee would be seeing him with someone who could be right for him. A woman who'd love him the way she did.

"What about your antique shop?" he asked. "You care about that store. It took you years to put everything together, and now you've added the Victorian Tea Room."

"I'll have to sell it—either that or close it down."

"But the women in town love your store!"

"Then perhaps one of them will be willing to purchase it."

"You don't mean it," Frank said again, his voice rising. "This is just another ploy to get me to change my mind and marry you."

That he would believe her capable of such a thing

hurt. "No, Frank, it's not. I'm contacting the real-estate people in the morning. Perhaps I shouldn't have mentioned it, but I felt you should know. Goodbye, Frank."

"I'm not going to marry you or anyone," he shouted as if she was hard of hearing.

"Yes, you've made that quite clear." At this point, if he *had* experienced a sudden change of heart, Dovie wasn't sure she'd agree to marry him, anyway.

CAL WASN'T HAPPY with the idea of finding Bitter End and he wouldn't be going there now, but for Jane.

He drove into Promise, hoping that when he arrived she'd have changed her mind, but one look told him he might as well save his breath. Jane opened the front door, and when she saw him, practically launched herself into his arms.

"I'm so excited!" she said, hugging him.

It was beginning to feel damn good to hold her. Beginning, hell, it felt like this was exactly where she belonged. Once again Cal forced himself to remember that Jane would put in her stint here, but when her three years were up, she'd return to California.

"I spent part of the morning with Savannah," he said, and withdrew a slip of paper from his shirt pocket. "She drew me a map showing us how to get to Bitter End."

"That's wonderful!"

Cal didn't agree.

"You're sure you'd rather drive?" She sounded

disappointed that they wouldn't be going on horse-back.

"I'm sure." He spread the map on top of the coffee table for her to examine.

She pored over it and then smiled up at him with such enthusiasm it was difficult not to feel some excitement himself. The problem was, Jane didn't understand what she was asking of him, and he couldn't find the words to explain it.

He'd seen the ghost town once, and that was all it had taken for him to know he never wanted to go back there. As teenagers, he and Glen and Grady had happened to overhear a conversation between his parents and the Westons. They'd been intrigued. Just as Jane was now.

They'd come up with a scheme to locate Bitter End on their own. The adventure had appealed to them; the secrecy, too.

Cal remembered that he'd been the skeptical one of the bunch. He wasn't sure he believed such a place existed. Glen seemed convinced the ghost town was there. Grady was undecided.

In the end it was Glen who turned out to be right. The old town was hidden deep in the hills, just as his parents had said. At first the three of them had been ecstatic, jumping up and down, congratulating each other. Cal remembered thinking that someone would probably include their names in a history book or a magazine article—as the boys who'd found a lost ghost town. Someone might even in-terview them for television.

None of that had happened—and for a reason. Not one of them ever mentioned finding Bitter End to any of their peers and certainly not to their parents. In fact, they'd never mentioned it again—until recently.

It was almost as though they'd made a secret pact not to discuss what they'd found, but that hadn't been the case. They didn't talk about it because they weren't sure what had happened or how to explain it.

All Cal could recall was how uncomfortable he'd been. How the feelings, of fear and oppressiveness, had overwhelmed him. The others had reacted the same way. After less than ten minutes all three had hightailed it out of town as if the hounds of hell were in hot pursuit.

"Should I bring a sweater?" Jane asked.

"That's probably a good idea." Cal wished to hell he could talk her out of this, but since that wasn't likely, he was determined to be there with her.

"I brought along a camera, too," Jane said as she swung a backpack over her shoulder. "Mom asked me to get some pictures."

"You mentioned the town to your mother?"

"Wasn't I supposed to?"

Cal wasn't sure how to answer. "No one around here talks about it much."

"I know," she said with a certain exasperation. "I don't understand that."

"Perhaps you will once you've been there."

"I wish I knew why everyone's so secretive about this place."

Cal knew it wouldn't do any good to tell her. She'd soon discover the answer on her own.

The drive out of town went well enough. They discussed Savannah, who'd told Cal about her pregnancy. Cal was happy for her and Laredo. "I imagine Glen and Ellie will be thinking about children soon, too," he said. "I hope so."

"Cal, they're newlyweds."

"Yes, but if my mother'd had anything to say about it, Ellie would've gotten pregnant on their wedding night and delivered their first grandchild nine months and thirty seconds later."

Jane laughed softly. "Your mother is eager for grandchildren to spoil. So is mine."

Cal wasn't wading into those shark-infested waters, not for anything.

With the help of Savannah's map, they were able to locate the general vicinity of the town. It would have helped had the tire tracks not been washed away by the recent storm, but every now and then Cal recognized some landmark himself. It amazed him that the memory of these details hadn't been lost. Although it'd been years since his visit, Cal had repeated the journey in his mind many times since.

He parked the truck when they'd driven as far as possible.

"According to Savannah, we'll need to walk in from here."

"I'm ready."

Jane had dressed in khaki shorts, hiking boots and T-shirt; on his advice she'd also worn a hat. Cal held her hand as they climbed over the rocks and limestone ledge.

"There," he said, pointing as the town came into view below. Seeing it again stole his breath. The buildings, the way the streets were laid out, were almost exactly as he remembered, as though the years had stood still. The church, at the far end of town, still stood with its burned-out steeple. The graveyard was beside the church. Some of the buildings along the street were of sun-bleached wood, some of stone, now brown with age. Stores, a saloon, livery stable with a small corral, a mercantile and even a hotel. A corral was situated close to the hotel.

"This is incredible," Jane breathed, slipping the backpack from her shoulders. She pulled out her camera and began shooting. "I can't believe it's here like this...."

Once she'd finished snapping pictures, Jane scrambled forward, bounding energetically over the rocks. Cal followed close behind, watching her, waiting for her reaction once she felt it.

He experienced the first sensation, a feeling of darkness and desolation, when they stepped onto the main street of Bitter End. Jane apparently did, too, because she stopped cold and slowly turned to face Cal. A puzzled frown appeared on her face.

"What *is* that?" she asked, lowering her voice to a whisper.

"What?" he asked, although he knew.

"This...this feeling."

"I don't know."

"You said this place was evil. I didn't know what you meant."

"I wasn't sure how to say it," Cal told her. But he could find no other word to describe what he and the others had experienced that day.

Jane's grip on his hand tightened as they made their way down the middle of the street. "It's growing stronger," she said in a weak whisper. "Do you feel it, too?"

"I feel it." The sensation grew heavier and more intense with each step they advanced.

"Look!" Jane said, gesturing at a rocking chair outside the saloon.

"What?"

"There's a guitar there."

"A guitar?" It took Cal a moment to see it, propped against the wall.

"That doesn't look like an antique, does it?" Jane said.

Cal went to investigate. He climbed the two short steps onto the boardwalk and reached for the guitar.

"Is it old?" Jane asked.

"This is no antique," Cal said, and frowned. Furthermore it was familiar. Where had he seen this guitar before? For the life of him, he couldn't remember.

"Cal, look!"

She was halfway down the street when Cal glanced up. He set the guitar down and raced after her. She was just outside what had once been the mercantile.

"What is it?" he asked.

She held up a half-full can of soda. "Someone's been here recently," she said.

He nodded. "Very recently." He was ready to leave even if she wasn't.

"Let's get out of here," Jane said.

Cal grabbed her hand and they turned to go back the same way they'd come in.

It wasn't until they passed the livery stable that they heard it. A moaning sound, coming from the hotel where Cal had stood only a minute or two ago.

Jane tensed and so did Cal. "What's that?" she whispered. "I didn't think I believed in ghosts, but..."

Cal had a sinking suspicion it wasn't a ghost. All at once he remembered where he'd last seen that guitar.

Bitter End didn't have ghosts, but it appeared to be populated by a single rat.

Chapter Eight

Savannah loved visiting Dovie's antique shop with its storehouse of treasures from earlier times. This particular visit was special for another reason—she planned to tell Dovie about the baby. Since Dr. Dickinson had confirmed her pregnancy, the knowledge that her child, Laredo's child, was growing inside her occupied more and more of her thoughts.

Dovie Boyd glanced up from behind the glass counter that displayed some of the shop's pricier antique china and jewelry.

"Savannah, my dear." Dovie's greeting held her usual graciousness and warmth. "It's good to see you."

"It's always a pleasure, Dovie." Savannah noticed that her friend was pale this morning. Come to think of it, she'd seemed tired and listless for a while now. Savannah assumed that had something to do with her separation from Frank Hennessey, although Dovie had never discussed it.

"Can I help you find something?" Dovie asked, stepping around the glass counter.

"I'm looking for something special," Savannah

said, placing her hand on her abdomen, "for our baby's nursery." She waited for Dovie's reaction.

"I don't have much in the way of—" Dovie stopped midsentence and stared at Savannah, her eyes brightening. "So *that's* what's different."

"You noticed already?" Savannah was only about two months along. It didn't seem possible that anyone would be able to detect the pregnancy this soon.

"In your eyes," Dovie explained. "You're fairly glowing with happiness." She smiled. "I know it's a cliché—that pregnant women have a glow about them—but like most clichés it has a basis in truth."

Some days it was all Savannah could do not to burst into tears when she thought about all the wonderful changes that had taken place in her life this past year. The afternoon she'd found the ghost town and dug up the White Lady Banks roses in the church cemetery had forever changed her life. It was on the return drive that she'd seen Laredo Smith walking along the side of the road. To this day she didn't know what had possessed her to stop and offer him a ride. She'd never done anything like that before or since. Within a few months she'd become Laredo's wife and now they were expecting a child.

"I *am* happy," Savannah said.

"You're radiant." They hugged, and as the older woman pulled away, Savannah noticed again how drawn Dovie looked.

"You haven't been ill, have you, Dovie?" she asked, deciding she should ask, just to be sure.

"No. I just haven't been sleeping well." She

managed a smile and continued, "I have some news, too."

Savannah had already heard that Mary Patterson had talked Dovie into a cruise; she was delighted. Dovie could use a vacation, however short, and her absence might clarify a thing or two in Frank's mind. Dovie was a remarkable woman, and if Frank Hennessey didn't realize it, then the sheriff was more of a fool than she'd thought. But she knew Frank almost as well as she did Dovie and suspected that the problem, whatever it was, would soon be resolved.

"I've decided to sell the house." Dovie's announcement was inflated with forced enthusiasm. "I'm going to be moving."

"Moving," Savannah repeated, trying to conceal her shock.

"I talked to a real-estate agent this morning and I'll be listing the house this afternoon. I'm...not sure just yet what I'll do about the business."

Speechless, Savannah needed time to recover.

"I know this comes as a surprise," Dovie said.

"Where will you go?" Savannah asked, when in reality her question should have been *why* Dovie would go. Why she'd consider leaving Promise. This was her home. She was an essential part of this community, loved by everyone here. Her shop was the very heart of the town, a mingling of past and present, a constant reminder of the heritage that made Promise special to those who lived there.

"I've decided to do some traveling," Dovie said, again with an eagerness that rang false. "I'm going to explore the world."

"The world…"

"The United States, at any rate. I understand that Charleston's lovely, and I've never seen New York. I've never seen the Rockies…" Her voice tapered off.

This was more than Savannah could take in. She felt the sudden need to sit down. "I realize it's a bit early for tea, but perhaps you wouldn't mind putting on a pot?"

"Of course."

While Dovie fussed with the tea, Savannah contemplated what she should say. She thought about her own relationship with Laredo, remembering how she'd felt when he returned to Oklahoma and she didn't believe she'd see him again. She'd made changes in her life, too, needing to do *something* to combat the terrible pain of his leaving. The changes hadn't been drastic, although Grady and a few others had behaved as though they no longer knew her. Cutting her hair was a small thing. Dovie planned on packing up her fifty-seven years of life and leaving everything that was familiar.

Savannah noticed that her friend's hand trembled as she poured the tea.

"Why would you leave here?" Savannah asked gently. "I'd like to know the real reason you'd consider moving away from Promise."

Dovie lowered her eyes and folded her hands in her lap. She didn't say anything for several tense moments. "Frank's dating Tammy Lee now and I can't bear—"

"Frank and Tammy Lee?" Savannah interrupted. She could hardly believe her ears. What man in his right mind would prefer that…that trashy Tammy Lee over Dovie?

"If it isn't Tammy Lee, it'll soon be someone else and…I can't abide seeing him fall in love with someone else." Dovie pulled a limp lace-bordered handkerchief from her pocket and dabbed her eyes.

Savannah leaned forward, hugging the woman who'd been both friend and substitute mother to her. She sympathized with the pain Dovie felt and wished there was something she could say or do that would ease her broken heart.

"Obviously I gave Frank more credit for intelligence than he deserves," Savannah snapped. The next time she saw him, she'd give him a tongue-lashing he wouldn't soon forget.

Dovie quickly composed herself, clearly embarrassed by her show of emotion. "It isn't such a bad thing, my leaving Promise," she said on a more cheerful note. "I'm actually looking forward to traveling. Eventually, I'm sure I'll find someplace in Montana or Colorado that reminds me of Promise. I'll settle right in and make a new life for myself." Her enthusiasm appeared more genuine this time. Savannah hated the thought of losing Dovie, especially for a reason as *stupid* as Frank Hennessey's stubborn pride.

She was about to say something else when an antique doll caught her eye. Faded and tattered, it sat on the edge of a dresser. Dovie's gaze followed hers.

"Do you recognize the doll?" Dovie asked. "Jane Dickinson brought it in and asked me about it. Apparently someone brought it into her office and asked her to find the owner. It's quite old and rather fragile. Have you ever seen it before?''

Savannah walked over to look at the antique doll. She picked it up and carefully examined its faded embroidered face. The button eyes seemed to stare back at her. "I've never seen anything like this."

"Me, neither." Dovie shook her head.

"But…it looks like something that might have come from Bitter End."

"Bitter End. That's what I thought," Dovie said excitedly.

"But how would anyone have gotten hold of it?" Savannah asked.

"Your guess is as good as mine." Dovie frowned. "Apparently whoever gave the doll to Jane—she couldn't tell me who—did so because he or she felt guilty about taking it."

"Why would anyone give it to…" Savannah paused.

"I suspect it was a child," Dovie said thoughtfully.

"I was thinking that very thing," Savannah murmured.

"It's highly unlikely that any child's been to Bitter End, though," Dovie pointed out. "Other than a handful of people, who even knows about the town?"

All at once everything fell into place. "*Richard* knows about Bitter End," Savannah said intently. "And he kidnapped Maggie for several hours, remember? What if he took her to Bitter End? He could've either given the doll to Maggie in an attempt to buy her silence or else Maggie took it without him knowing.''

''Someone needs to ask Maggie about this,'' Dovie said.

Her thoughts were a reflection of Savannah's own. Maggie had refused to talk about the time she'd been missing, despite numerous efforts by a number of people, herself included. Even knowing what she did about her brother, Savannah couldn't believe Richard would intentionally take the child. Everyone had been terribly worried—no one more than Savannah, whose fears had been compounded by guilt. The child had been in her care when she disappeared, and Savannah had blamed herself.

Then early the next morning Maggie had come running down the driveway. For the rest of her life, Savannah would remember the way Grady had raced toward the child. At that moment she'd realized how much her brother had come to love Maggie. He might not have fathered her, but he'd always be a real father to the little girl. She'd long had her suspicions about Maggie's biological father, but had kept those to herself.

''Perhaps Grady should be the one to ask Maggie about the doll,'' Savannah said. The little girl had refused to discuss where she'd been or who'd taken her, but she trusted Grady now and seemed willing to confide in him. Since she hadn't been physically harmed, Frank had felt they should count their blessings and leave it. He doubted Maggie would be able to help them locate Richard, anyway. However, that was before they knew about the doll.

''Someone should bring Frank into this, too,''

Dovie said. "I understand there's a warrant out for Richard's arrest..." Her voice faltered and she looked away. Whether her reaction was because of Frank or Richard, Savannah couldn't say.

"I'll have Grady call him."

For the next couple of hours Savannah was involved in talking to people. She'd contacted Jane Dickinson's office and learned that it was her day off. Apparently she'd gone somewhere with Cal Patterson.

Caroline agreed Grady would be the right person to discuss the matter of the doll with Maggie. Sheriff Hennessey was brought in, as well, and suggested they talk to her at the ranch house.

Savannah returned to the ranch, baked bread and mulled over what she'd learned from Dovie. She was also worried about Richard. She knew he had a rifle, but didn't like to think that her brother would intentionally hurt anyone. After these past few months, though, she couldn't predict what he might do.

When Caroline and Maggie arrived late in the afternoon, they all gathered in the living room, together with Frank Hennessey. Maggie stayed close to her mother, glancing nervously about the room. Grady held his arms open and Savannah was gratified to see the child willingly sit next to him.

Grady opened the bag Dovie had given Savannah and withdrew the old tattered doll. "Do you recognize this?" he asked Maggie.

The little girl took one look at it and covered her face with both hands. Her shoulders started to shake. "I'm sorry I stole her! I'm sorry!"

"But the doll said she was glad." Grady spoke with such gentle concern that Savannah wanted to kiss him. "She told me how grateful she was that she had someone to love her."

Maggie lowered her hands and gazed at him with searching eyes. "She told you that?"

Grady nodded gravely. "She came from the ghost town, didn't she?"

Maggie's hands flew back to her face. "I'm not supposed to tell!"

"It's all right, Maggie," Grady continued. "You won't be punished."

"But Richard said Mommy would die if I told anyone. He said I'd never see her again and that she'd bleed real bad."

Frank muttered a curse under his breath, and while Savannah wouldn't have used that precise language, she was in full agreement. That her brother would knowingly frighten the child in this manner was inexcusable. His one redeeming act had been to bring Maggie back. He'd stolen another truck shortly thereafter, but at least Maggie had been safely returned.

"Sometimes people say things that aren't true." Grady placed his arm around the child's shoulders, both shielding her and comforting her at once.

Maggie kept her head lowered, as though she felt undecided about what to do.

"Is Richard at the ghost town?" Caroline asked softly.

"Will you die if I tell?" Maggie asked her mother.

"No, sweetheart, I won't die." Caroline linked

her fingers with Grady's. "I'm going to marry Grady very soon and we'll all be very happy."

"Will you have other babies so I can be a big sister?"

Savannah watched as Caroline met Grady's eyes, then nodded. "Yes, sweetheart, you'll have plenty of opportunities to be a big sister."

"Can I really keep the doll?" Maggie asked next.

Grady raised the rag doll to his ear, his expression somber. Maggie watched his every move. Slowly, a bit at a time, Grady's mouth formed a smile. "She says she needs someone to love her and take care of her and be kind to her."

"I can do that," Maggie said with a questioning glance at her mother.

"She needs lots of tender loving care," Caroline added. "She's fragile and old."

"I'll take good care of her," Maggie promised. "I'll call her...Isabelle."

Grady handed her the doll, and Maggie pressed Isabelle against her shoulder and gently patted her back.

"I'm sorry Richard lied to you," Savannah felt obliged to say.

"I don't like Richard anymore," Maggie said.

"You don't need to worry about seeing him again," Frank Hennessey assured her. "Once I get my hands on him, he won't see the light of day for one hell of a long time."

"IN HERE." Cal's heart pounded as he peered into the hotel. The staircase had collapsed and he was able to make out a figure trapped beneath the boards. Richard Weston, he was sure.

Jane was a few steps behind Cal. They cautiously entered the hotel and began to approach the ruined stairs.

"Stand back," Cal ordered, looking up to make sure nothing else threatened to fall. As soon as he'd assured himself it was safe, he started to remove the boards.

It was indeed Richard, and his groans grew louder, more plaintive. He was in obvious pain and close to unconsciousness.

Jane checked his vital signs. "There's no telling how long he's been here."

"Two days," Richard whispered, his voice weak. "Am I going to die?"

"Not if I have anything to say about it," she said firmly.

Cal understood that to Jane, medicine was a passion the same way ranching was to him, and he respected her for it. *Loved* her for it. He loved her courage and her sense of humor, too, her honesty, her kindness. Why that realization should come to him at a time like this, he didn't know. He'd intended never to make himself vulnerable again after Jennifer had humiliated him in front of the entire town. But he loved Jane. He felt no doubt, not about her or his feelings.

He continued to lift the heavy pieces of wood that trapped the injured man. The way in which Richard's leg was twisted told him it was badly broken.

Richard was moaning for water. Jane carefully

lifted his head and dribbled liquid between his parched lips.

"Don't let me die," Richard pleaded between swallows. "Tell my mother I'm not ready."

Jane raised her gaze to Cal's.

"His mother died more than six years ago," he told her.

"He's hallucinating," she explained. "We need to get him out of here. The sooner the better."

"How?" The truck was parked some distance away, and Cal was aware it would be nearly impossible to move him.

"He's lost consciousness," Jane said.

"His right leg's broken."

"I suspect internal injuries, as well."

"How are we going to transport him?" Cal asked, seeking her advice. His biggest fear was that moving Richard, especially in his frail condition, might kill him. Cal didn't need Richard Weston's death on his conscience.

"We have to get help," Jane said, and while her voice was calm, he sensed the urgency in her words. "Leave me here and go back to town. Have Sheriff Hennessey call for a medevac. His injuries are far too extensive for me to handle. He's going to have to be airlifted out of here."

"You'll be all right alone?" he asked, getting to his feet.

She nodded, then looked up at him. "Hurry," she said. "I don't think he'll last much longer."

Cal sprinted out of the hotel, running through the brush and up the hill as fast as he could force his legs to move. He didn't like the idea of leaving Jane in Bitter End, but he didn't have a choice.

By the time he reached the pickup, he was panting and breathless. Sweat poured off his brow as he leaped into the cab and fired the engine to life.

He drove to the highway at a speed far too great for the terrain, and the truck's jolting threw him repeatedly and painfully against the door. Bruises, however, were a small price to pay for saving a man's life.

No sooner had he reached the highway than two patrol cars came into view, their lights flashing. Cal pressed his hand on the horn and slammed on the brakes. He screeched to a stop, swerving partway into the other lane.

Frank Hennessey was out of his patrol car in seconds. "This damn well better be good," he yelled.

"Richard Weston," Cal said, hopping out of the pickup. "At Bitter End. He's injured badly."

To Cal's surprise Savannah and Grady got out of the patrol car, as well.

"So he's holed up in Bitter End?" The question came from Grady.

"Yes. Jane and I were there. We found him. Apparently he was on the stairway in the hotel when it collapsed. He's in bad shape—broken leg, internal injuries."

"Oh, no!" Savannah covered her mouth.

"We shouldn't try to move him. We'll need to arrange for a chopper—he's got to be airlifted out."

Frank was already reaching for his radio, barking out orders.

Cal felt Savannah studying him. All he could say was, "Jane's there. She knows what to do."

He wanted to reassure Savannah that everything would be fine, but he couldn't. He had no way of knowing what had happened since he left the town. From what he'd seen of Richard, and from what Jane had said, it didn't look promising. Cal knew that despite the things her brother had done, Savannah still loved him.

"How is he really?" Grady asked him privately.

"Not good." No point hiding the truth from Grady. They'd been friends since childhood, and Grady counted on him for the truth. "I don't know if he's going to make it, so prepare yourself for the worst."

Grady nodded and moved away. "Maybe it'd be best if we called in Wade McMillen," he said, wiping one hand down his face. "If there's time..."

Grady wanted to give his brother the chance to make his peace with God. Cal had his doubts. Richard had always been unrepentant. Worse, he was unconscious, possibly dying, and nothing short of a miracle would save him now.

Cal suspected that the following hours would repeat themselves in his mind for years to come. Because of the fresh tire tracks left in the soft ground, Cal was able to lead Sheriff Hennessey, Grady and Savannah to Bitter End. The second patrol car returned to Promise for Wade McMillen. If Richard wasn't in need of the pastor's comfort, then Savannah and Grady would be.

Cal's biggest concern wasn't for Richard. Instead, his thoughts were on Jane. He'd hated like hell to leave her, knowing how uneasy she'd felt in the ghost town. Damn Richard Weston. If he died, leaving Jane alone with a dead man in the middle of that empty town, he'd never forgive the bastard.

As it turned out, Richard was still clinging to life when they reached Bitter End. Grady and Savannah immediately besieged Jane with questions about their brother.

Cal stepped out of the way and watched as Jane skillfully reassured them. She'd been busy while he was away, Cal noticed. Even without medical equipment, Jane had worked to save Richard Weston's life. She'd created a makeshift splint for his leg and managed to shift him onto his side. She'd monitored his pulse and his breathing.

Frank put out a red flare for the helicopter, and it seemed no time at all before he heard the distinctive sound of the blades.

With Jane's help, the medics loaded Richard onto a stretcher and hooked him up to an emergency oxygen supply. Cal and Frank cleared a path, then Richard was carried to the helicopter.

His injuries were determined to be too extensive for the hospital in Brewster, and he was transported to Austin, instead. If he lasted that long, Cal thought grimly. It would be touch and go.

Because of the limited space aboard the helicopter, Jane wouldn't be traveling with them.

They all stood back as the chopper rose, carrying Richard Weston away. Cal placed his arm around Jane's shoulders and felt her trembling.

"Whatever happens is out of my hands now," she whispered.

Cal pressed his chin against the top of her head. "You did everything you could."

"I know." She glanced up and down the streets of Bitter End. "I don't want to come back here," she said with vehemence. "Ever!"

Cal couldn't agree with her more.

IT WAS A DAY Frank Hennessey would long remember. Richard Weston, if he lived, faced twenty years behind bars without the possibility of parole. Richard deserved that prison sentence, but Frank felt badly for Grady and Savannah.

Wade McMillen had counseled both of them. Frank never had been one to attend church, but he liked and respected Reverend McMillen. As long as Wade didn't preach at him, then Frank wouldn't quote the law at him, either. In a situation like this, he figured, the reverend provided a service nobody else could. Including the sheriff.

Frank was with the brother and sister when the phone rang about eight that night. Grady leaped on it, and after the initial greeting, glanced across the room where Savannah sat with Laredo.

He nodded and murmured a handful of thank-yous before replacing the receiver. "That was the hospital in Austin," Grady announced. His words had everyone's attention.

"He's going to make it," Grady said, and his voice cracked. When Caroline put her arm around him, Grady clung to her tightly.

Savannah burst into tears and hugged her husband.

Frank didn't want to be the one to remind them

that once Richard had recovered, he'd be placed in a maximum-security prison. If Frank hadn't disliked the man already, what Richard had said to Maggie to prevent her telling anyone where she'd been would have done it.

Since the deputy who'd driven Wade McMillen out to the Yellow Rose had already left, Frank drove the reverend back to town.

They chatted amicably, sharing insights and theories about the youngest Weston's personality. Frank dropped Wade off, then, on impulse, drove past Dovie's house.

He wasn't sure what he intended to do. Probably nothing. A few weeks ago he would've been spending this night with her. She would probably have waited up for him, brewing a pot of coffee in case he wanted to talk, which he almost always did. He missed those times with Dovie.

Despite everything, he missed her more rather than less with each day that passed. As he'd expected, her lights were out. She might be asleep—or on that cruise she'd mentioned. He'd forgotten the exact date she was supposed to go—although Louise Powell and Tammy Lee could no doubt have told him.

With a heavy heart he turned the corner, and that was when he saw the Realtor's sign. His heart felt as if it'd taken a ten-story tumble. She hadn't been bluffing when she said she'd leave Promise. He stared at the sign, shaken and hurt, trying to imagine Promise without Dovie.

Two days later Frank sat in the café at the bowling alley drinking a mug of coffee. His dour mood had kept his friends at bay. Anyone looking for idle conversation sought out someone else.

He noticed with something of a shock that Wade McMillen had slipped into the seat across from him.

Frank scowled. "I don't remember asking for company."

"You didn't, but I decided to join you, anyway." Wade raised his hand to attract the waitress's attention. Neither spoke again until she'd brought his coffee.

"Look, if you're interested in scintillating conversation, I'd be happy to steer you elsewhere. I'm not in the mood."

"So I noticed, Sheriff. Something on your mind?"

He had to give the preacher credit for guts. "As it happens, there is."

"Want to talk about it?"

"Not particularly."

Wade studied him. "I don't suppose this has something to do with Dovie Boyd."

"Why? Did she come and cry on your shoulder?" Frank muttered angrily.

"Nope. Dovie didn't say a word."

"Then how'd you know?"

Wade smiled, and it was the knowing grin of an observant man. "You might say *you* told me, Frank."

"Me?"

"You've been down in the mouth for weeks. The way I figure it, you can trust me enough to help or you can sit in the café and stare at the wall."

"Is it that obvious?"

"Yup."

Wade certainly didn't pull his punches, Frank thought. "It's not going to do any good to discuss it. My mind's made up. Besides, I already know what you're going to say."

"Do you, now." The knowing smile was back in place.

If Frank hadn't liked the other man so much, he might have been irritated. "You're a preacher."

"Yes, but I'm also a man," Wade told him.

Frank sighed deeply. "Dovie wants me to marry her."

"And you don't love her?"

"Wrong," he snapped. "I love her so damn much I can hardly think straight anymore. We had a good thing, the two of us. I spent the night with her a couple times a week, and we had one of the best damn relationships I've ever had. I always had this sort of vague thought that one day we'd get married—and then I realized I couldn't. I just could not go through with it," he said slowly, shaking his head. "As soon as I told her the truth, it was over. Just like that. Hell, if I'd lied to her, she'd never have known the difference. A lot of good being honest did me." He suspected his words had shocked the minister, and that was exactly what he wanted. To Frank's surprise Wade didn't so much as blink.

"You love her, but you don't want to marry her."

"Yes," Frank said more loudly than he intended.

"Any reason?"

"I've got a long list," Frank muttered.

"I'm not going anywhere," Wade said.

Frank wished he would. Wade McMillen wasn't

going to tell him anything he didn't already know. He wasn't going to offer a quick solution to a complex problem. If anything, he'd make Frank feel even guiltier for not marrying Dovie.

"You enjoy your freedom," Wade said. "A man who's been a bachelor all these years is set in his ways."

"Exactly." Frank was impressed at Wade's understanding. "I happen to like the way I live, and much as I love Dovie, I don't want a woman messing with how I do things."

"I'm a bachelor myself," Wade reminded him.

"If I want to belch after dinner, I don't need to worry about offending a woman. I can hang around the house in my underwear if I feel like it. I can pile up all my papers and magazines and read them all at once without hearing about the mess."

"I know what you mean."

"If my dirty clothes litter the floor for a couple days, I won't have someone picking them up for me and then complaining about it."

"That's what I'm like, too," Wade said, "but it does get lonely every now and then."

"Damn lonely," Frank agreed. And nothing helped. The dinner date with Tammy Lee had been a disaster, one that wouldn't be repeated. The only woman he wanted was Dovie.

"I'm going to lose her, Wade," he said, staring into his coffee. "She's put her house up for sale."

"So I understand."

"There's no solution. Either I change who I am or I let her walk out of my life."

"And both of those prospects are making you un- happy. It's eating you up inside."

"I might as well be drinking acid," Frank con- fessed. The knot in his stomach had become per- manent. Even when he went to bed at night, he couldn't make himself relax. He used to fall asleep the instant his head hit the pillow. No longer. His mind constantly churned with the two miserable al- ternatives—marriage or no Dovie.

"There's no solution," he muttered again.

"I wouldn't say that," Wade countered. "Some- times people are so caught up in the problem the obvious answer escapes them."

Frank raised his gaze to meet Wade's.

"There's a reason I came to talk to you," Wade continued. "I've got an idea," he said, steepling his fingers in front of him. "One that'll give you both what you're looking for."

Chapter Nine

Dusk settled comfortably over the Yellow Rose Ranch. Caroline stood on the porch, savoring the beauty of the sunset and the peace of a Sunday evening. Within minutes the moon would rise to greet her, and a million twinkling stars would nod their welcome.

Grady joined her, standing behind her to slip his arms around her waist. In less than a week they would become husband and wife. As the wedding approached, Caroline tried not to become sidetracked by the events concerning Richard. He'd robbed her and Grady of so much already. All she wanted now was to blend her life with Grady's.

"I thought I'd find you out here," he whispered close to her ear.

She hugged his arms. "I needed a moment of solitude."

"We both do." Grady exhaled slowly. "So much has happened in the past few days it's hard to take it all in."

Savannah and Laredo had moved into their new home. At the same time, Caroline and Maggie had made the transition from their rented house in the city to the ranch house with Grady. They'd spent all day hauling boxes from one place to the other. Later in the afternoon Laredo and Savannah had driven to Austin to visit Richard and had yet to return.

"Maggie's asleep," Grady said, nuzzling her neck.

Caroline closed her eyes, cherishing these moments alone with the man she loved. It was a rare pleasure these last hectic days before the wedding.

"I'm looking forward to just the two of us being together," she told him. Away from the worries about Richard, the wedding, the hard work of merging one household with another. They'd decided to take a four-day honeymoon in New Orleans, and just then, getting away seemed to Caroline like a small slice of heaven.

"You're not the only one anticipating our honeymoon!" Grady chuckled softly. "It's beginning to feel like Grand Central Station around here."

"This time next week I'll be your wife."

"And I'll be your husband," Grady said, as if he still had trouble thinking of himself that way. "I swear there's something happening in Promise this year."

"How do you mean?"

"All the weddings." Grady sounded incredulous. "It started with Savannah and Laredo."

"Then Ellie and Glen."

"Now it'll be us."

"I have a sneaking suspicion who's going to be next." Caroline nudged Grady lightly with her elbow. "Cal and Jane." She'd watched them the day

Richard was discovered in Bitter End and recognized the signs. She suspected they were only now becoming aware of their feelings for each other. Caroline had noticed something else, too—the rough edges of Cal's personality seemed to be wearing smooth. Perhaps even more telling were the changes Caroline had noticed in Jane. The California native had become one of them. A Texan at heart.

The last time Ellie had stopped by the post office to collect her mail, she'd mentioned that Cal was giving Jane horseback-riding lessons. Caroline would bet that the good doctor was becoming familiar with more than horses. Jane Dickinson had the look. "Yes," she said softly. "Cal and Jane."

"You're suggesting Cal's in love?" Grady shook his head. "No way!"

"We'll see," Caroline said confidently. "I wouldn't be surprised if they announced their engagement before the end of the year."

Grady responded by snickering in her ear. "Boy, are you off base with that one. Cal and I've been best friends for years. If he was thinking of getting married, don't you think he'd mention it to me?"

"Not necessarily."

"You don't know Cal and me—we're like this." He crossed two fingers and waved them under her nose. "Close."

"Uh-huh."

"So," Grady said with conviction, "if Cal was interested in a woman, I'd be the first to know. We don't have secrets from each other."

"Oh, really?" Caroline tried but couldn't keep the sarcasm out of her voice.

"Damn straight."

"Then answer me this," she said, smugly. "When did you tell Cal you were in love with me?"

His silence was answer enough.

"Well, I'm waiting." She turned to face him, hooked her arms around his neck and tilted back her head to get a good look at his face.

Grady's eyes avoided hers. "That's not a fair question."

"Why isn't it?"

"Because…well, because it took me a long time to figure out how I felt about you and even longer to act on it. That being the case, I couldn't very well say anything to Cal."

Caroline rolled her eyes for effect.

"Hey," Grady argued, "the man is always the last to know."

Her cocky grin was wasted on him. "My point exactly. Cal won't mention his feelings for Jane until he's ready to put an engagement ring on her finger. Trust me on this, Weston."

"Is that right," he muttered.

"That's right."

"And how did you get so smart?"

"Practice," she teased, and kissed the corner of his mouth. "Lots and lots of practice."

His eyes grew dark and sexy as he focused his gaze on her lips. Slowly he lowered his mouth to hers in a kiss that was open, purposeful and hungry.

The kiss was wonderful. Being right was nice— but not nearly as satisfying as two minutes in the arms of the man she loved.

JANE SAT AT HER DESK reviewing her appointment schedule for the following day. She was nearly finished and eager to escape the office for her next riding lesson. In truth it was Cal she really wanted to see, not Atta Girl, fond though she was of the horse. They'd been making steady progress, and when she arrived these days, it wasn't unusual for Atta Girl to gallop to the fence to greet her.

The time Jane spent at the ranch had lengthened to include dinner on her lesson days. Since Cal wouldn't accept payment for teaching her to ride, she'd taken it upon herself to cook his meal afterward. She experimented with traditional Texas recipes, but introduced some "California cuisine," too.

More and more Jane found herself looking forward to being with Cal. This evening she planned to create a special meal, complete with birthday cake and candles. Cal had no way of knowing it was her birthday—but he was the person she wanted to spend it with.

"Do you need anything else?" Jenny Bender, her receptionist, asked a few minutes later.

"Not a thing, Jenny, thanks—and thanks again for the flowers." How Jenny had learned about her birthday, Jane could only guess.

"I'll be heading out, then," Jenny said. "The answering service is on."

As soon as Jane was finished, she locked up the clinic and hurried to her house. The white lab coat was replaced with a freshly laundered snap shirt, and her skirt with comfortable slim-leg jeans. Cal had found an old pair of chaps and she strapped those on over the jeans, then reached for her hat and gloves. She was two minutes from walking out when she heard the doorbell.

Groaning inwardly at the delay, Jane answered the door.

"Surprise!" Her mother and father stood on the other side, their faces revealing guileless pleasure at surprising her.

"Happy birthday, darling," her mother said.

Jane stood there, too shocked to do anything more than stare.

"My goodness," her father said. "Look at you!"

Jane hugged her mother and kissed her father's cheek. "What do you think?" she asked, and whirled around to let them have the full effect of her transformation.

"I love it!" her mother cried.

"Cowboy chic," her father added with a grin.

Jane brought them both into the living room. "What are you doing in Texas?"

"Your father's attending a conference in Oklahoma City starting on Wednesday. We decided that since we were going to be this close, it'd only be a hop, skip and a jump to come by and surprise you for your birthday."

Jane had to admit she was surprised, all right.

"We've come to take you to dinner," her father said. He handed her an envelope, which she knew contained a check. "Happy birthday, honey."

"Thanks, Dad, Mom. I can't believe you're really here!" She took a deep breath. "Where are you staying?"

"Your father found a quaint little bed-and-breakfast place here in town."

"Cal's parents own that," Jane said excitedly.

"The same Cal you've been telling us about?" Her mother raised her eyebrows.

"One and the same. Mom, Dad, would you mind if I invited him to join us? I don't know if he can, since it's such short notice, but I do want you to meet him."

"A cowboy?" her father asked.

"One of the best you're likely to meet," she said. "A *real* cowboy."

"You're not falling in love with him, are you?"

"Dad, please! I'm a big girl now and I can make my own decisions."

"Fine, but remember you belong in California, not Texas."

Jane's excitement dimmed as she felt the pressure building inside her. From the time she'd been accepted into medical school, everyone had assumed she'd join her uncle's practice. Everyone including Jane. She wasn't so sure anymore. Cal had said that once her commitment to the government was satisfied, he knew she'd return to California. She'd neither confirmed nor denied it. She couldn't, because she didn't know herself. She knew what was expected of her, but her heart had begun to tell her something different. She loved her work at the clinic. It had taken time and effort to become part of this community, and now that she'd established friendships, she didn't want to leave. Nothing needed to be decided right now, she realized that. But the reminder was one she'd rather ignore, especially since she'd never mentioned her uncle Ken to Cal.

"Is this what you've been wearing for your riding lessons?" her mother wanted to know.

She nodded, proud of her accomplishments.

"Don't get too acclimatized," her father said in a heavyhanded attempt to humor that did nothing to disguise his message.

"Dad, would you stop? I'll be back in just a minute," she said. The phone in the kitchen offered some privacy. She punched out Cal's number and waited through four long rings before he answered.

"You're coming, aren't you?" he asked immediately.

"I can't."

"Why not?"

It thrilled her to hear how disappointed he sounded. "My parents arrived unexpectedly to take me to dinner. They'd like to meet you," she said, stretching the truth, but only a little. "Can you drive into town and join us at the Chili Pepper?"

He hesitated, then said, "I'll need an hour before I can get there."

"We'll wait," she promised, eager for her family to meet the man who'd come to mean so much to her.

When she hung up, Jane discovered that her mother had entered the kitchen. Impulsively Jane hugged her.

"You're happy, aren't you?" Stephanie Dickinson observed.

Jane knew that her parents had worried about her move to Texas, especially in the beginning before she'd made friends. It was the first time she'd lived more than an hour from her family home, the first time she'd been so completely on her own.

"I'm anxious for you to meet Cal," she said, clasping both her mother's hands. She wanted this meeting to go well on both sides, although she wasn't ready to share her feelings for Cal with anyone yet, not even her mother.

"Didn't you say his parents are the owners of the bed-and-breakfast? They certainly seem like nice people. They're packing for a cruise, and apparently they leave in the morning."

"They're wonderful." So was Cal, but she didn't mention that. Jane had met Mary and Phil the night she'd first played bingo and had seen them a number of times since. They were warm gracious folk whose personalities were perfectly suited to operating a bed-and-breakfast.

"You're not really serious about this cowpoke, are you?" her father asked, entering the kitchen.

"Daddy!"

"Don't go losing your heart to a cowboy," her father teased, kissing her soundly on both cheeks. "I can't get over the sight of you in all this cowboy gear. I don't know if I'd have recognized you."

Smiling, Jane went along with his silliness, realizing suddenly how much she missed her parents. She knew her dad could be a little too obvious in his remarks; she also knew he loved her and cared about her welfare.

After changing out of the riding clothes and into a skirt and sweater, she brewed a pot of coffee. The three of them sat in the living room visiting while they waited for Cal. Jane showed them her photographs of Bitter End, and they enjoyed a vigorous discussion of theories about its abandonment.

The instant the doorbell chimed Jane was on her feet. She was unaccountably nervous about Cal's meeting her parents.

"Hi," he said in his soft Texas drawl.

"Hi," Jane returned, and held open the screen door for him. Cal looked incredibly attractive, in jeans, polished boots, a white Western shirt and tweed jacket; she'd hardly ever seen him so formally dressed. Since their trip to Bitter End, her feelings for him had solidified. He'd been supportive and helpful, and later, after Richard Weston was airlifted to the hospital in Austin, he'd sat and talked with her. Among other things, he'd told her about Richard Weston's family history. His willingness to do this, to share a part of himself and his community, revealed that he'd come to trust her. It meant more to her than fifty riding lessons and a hundred bingo wins.

"Mom, Dad," she said, taking Cal by the hand and leading him into the room. "This is Cal Patterson."

Her father stood and the two of them exchanged hearty handshakes. Cal held a bouquet of flowers in his left hand, which he gave to her mother.

"You mean to say those aren't for me?" Jane teased, setting her hands on her hips in mock outrage.

Cal flashed her a sexy grin and she blushed. Jane could actually feel the heat enter her cheeks. Only one man was capable of doing this to her, and that was Cal.

"I thought we'd take Mom and Dad to the Chili Pepper," Jane said. "It's the best barbecue in town," she explained to her parents.

"Great. A chance to taste authentic Texas barbecue," her father said jovially.

"Do they have a low-fat menu?" her mother asked.

"No." Jane was adamant. "And don't ask for dressing on the side, either."

"But, Jane—"

"Mother, trust me on this."

"All right, all right," her mother said.

Although the restaurant was only a few blocks away, her father insisted on driving. Since Cal and Jane had been in to eat a couple of times, the hostess greeted them by name and led them to a booth.

"The music's a little loud, isn't it?" her father complained the minute they were seated.

"They like it that way here," Jane said.

"That country music's got a real twang to it." Her mother grimaced as if she could barely stand to hear it.

"I was afraid you were going to develop an accent," her father added, "and you'd end up sounding like that girl who's singing now."

Jane offered Cal an apologetic smile, trying to convey that her parents didn't mean to be condescending. He nodded reassuringly.

A Willie Nelson song came on, and as usual, everyone in the restaurant sang along, Jane included. Her parents lowered their menus and stared, transfixed by the boisterous songfest. The instant the tune ended, patrons and waiters went about their business again.

"This is Willie Nelson country," Jane explained.

"Everyone in California feels the same way about the Beach Boys," her mother said.

"Although I wouldn't call them *boys* anymore," her father put in, and this time Cal and Jane both laughed.

They ordered their drinks—beer for everyone except Stephanie who was having iced tea, "with fresh lemons," she'd specified.

"Can't decide, Mom?" Jane asked.

"It's all...so..."

"Western," Jane supplied.

Her mother nodded.

"Mom, you aren't going to find nouvelle cuisine in Promise."

"Oh, all right," Stephanie Dickinson said with a sigh, closing her menu. "I'll have a salad. I just hope they serve a decent avocado."

It was all Jane could do not to groan out loud. Especially since she was uncomfortably reminded of her own attitude a few months ago.

Her father was the conversationalist in the family and he began telling a story about stopping at a service station in a small town outside San Antonio. "I asked this old geezer how far it was to Promise and he said—" her father paused for effect "—it was down yonder." He laughed until his eyes watered. "Then he corrected himself and said it was *way* down yonder."

Jane noted that Cal didn't laugh nearly as hard. "Dad," she said, "this *is* Texas."

"I know, I know. When in Rome—"

"Yes, Daddy."

Their meals arrived—three orders of barbecue and one green salad—and Jane relaxed as they began to eat.

"Did you know it's Jane's birthday?" her father asked when they were nearly finished.

"Dad!"

"As a matter of fact, I did," Cal said. He reached into his pocket and withdrew a small square box wrapped in white paper with a gold bow.

"Who told you?" Jane asked him.

He hesitated, then confessed, "Jenny."

"My receptionist," Jane told her parents.

"Aren't you going to open it?" her mother asked, eyeing the box.

"It's not an engagement ring, is it?" her father chided. "I don't want a cowpoke to steal my little girl's heart."

"Dad!" Jane hurriedly removed the paper. Inside the jeweler's box was a Black Hills gold necklace and gold chain. Jane lifted her gaze to Cal's. "Thank you," she whispered. "It's beautiful."

For a second it was only the two of them. His eyes held hers for the sweetest moment. "So are you," he said, for her ears only.

Jane removed the necklace from its cotton bed and Cal helped her put it on. When he'd finished, Jane noticed that her mother and father were watching them closely.

"So...you've adjusted to Texas?" her father asked unnecessarily.

"I like it here."

"Her attitude changed the night she won the Blackout Bingo jackpot," Cal told them.

"You played bingo?" Her mother looked aghast.

"We all do, just about every Friday night." Jane knew they didn't really understand that bingo was one of the few entertainment choices in a town the size of Promise.

"You're joking, I hope." This from her father.

"I bowl, too." Only once, but her family didn't have to know that.

Her mother gasped.

Jane laughed and squeezed Cal's hand. Oh, yes, their attitude was very much what her own had been like when she arrived here. She truly understood now, for the first time, why her reception in town had been cool. "It's another one of those when-in-Rome things."

"Just don't bring these Texas habits with you when you come home," her father said. "I can't imagine what Ken will think."

"Ken is Harry's brother," her mother explained. "Jane will be joining him at his medical clinic when she's finished her assignment here."

"Eventually he's going to make our little girl a full partner," her father said proudly, and smiled at her. Jane gave him a feeble smile in return, wishing they'd kept this information to themselves.

"I see," Cal said.

Jane felt him stiffen, and when she squeezed his hand again he didn't respond by squeezing her fingers back. She should have known this would happen, should have explained to Cal long before now about her uncle Ken. She would have, if she'd known what to say. Now he'd been hit with the information at the worst possible moment. She couldn't explain or reassure, not with her parents there. She'd lost her chance to tell him tactfully and in her own way.

They all rode back in the car to Jane's house, and her parents left shortly afterward, promising to stop by the health clinic the next morning, before they drove on to Oklahoma.

"I need to go, too," Cal said, disappointing Jane. She'd hoped they'd have some time alone together.

"You can't stay a few minutes?" she pressed.

"No."

"You'll phone later?" she asked as she walked him to the door.

"I'll try," he said noncommittally.

"I'd like to explain what my parents said about me joining my uncle Ken's medical practice. I apologize for not mentioning it sooner. Nothing's for sure yet, and—"

"We'll talk about that later."

"All right," she mumbled, her heart sinking. His look told her everything. He was angry now, and felt betrayed, and it would be best to let him sort through his feelings before they talked this out. "Thank you for the necklace," she told him, and despite his being upset with her, kissed him soundly on the lips.

HE REALLY KNEW how to pick 'em, Cal decided, not for the first time. Jennifer, and now Jane. He must have a weakness for deceptive city girls. At least he hadn't made the mistake this time of asking the woman to marry him.

From this point forward he was determined to avoid all women whose names started with the letter *J*.

Cal sat out on the porch in the moonlight and reviewed the evening. He'd been looking forward to meeting Jane's parents, but it hadn't taken him long to discover that the elder Dickinsons viewed him and the entire population of Promise as hicks. However, he could live with that. What he couldn't live with was Jane's plans to join her uncle's medical practice. She might have said something herself, and a hell of a lot sooner. He could only assume she'd kept the information from him on purpose. She intended to go back to California, just the way he'd claimed; it sounded as though her life was already planned for her. Planned years into the future, with no room for someone like him.

His forehead pounded with an increasingly painful headache. Cal walked inside and turned on the kitchen light. Obviously he needed to have his head examined. Not because of the headache, but because he was fool enough to make the same mistake twice. Only this time it hurt more.

This time his heart was fully involved and he'd started to dream again.

CAL EXPECTED Jane to show up the following afternoon and she did. A few minutes before five he heard the familiar sound of her car; fortifying himself, he stepped out of the barn, eager to get this confrontation over with.

"Hello," she called, closing her car door. She was dressed in her shirt and jeans and looked as brightly beautiful as a rodeo princess. He wanted to remember her like this.

"Hi," he said, keeping all emotion out of his voice.

"Thanks for being so patient with my parents last night," she said. "I can't believe some of the things they said."

They stood a few feet apart, a little awkwardly.

She sighed and glanced sheepishly at him. "I realized I sounded just like them not so long ago."

"You're right, you did." He wasn't going to disagree with her.

"But I came around, with a little help from my friends."

He nodded.

"Mostly from Dovie and you. Ellie, too."

He didn't respond.

"I'm here for my lesson," she said, as if she needed to remind him.

"I'm afraid there won't be one today."

Disappointment flashed from her eyes. "Oh."

"You should have phoned first."

"I...I..." She nodded. "You're right, I should have. Do you have time for a cup of coffee?"

His initial thought was to refuse her and hope she'd be smart enough to figure it out for herself. But he suspected it would take more than the cold shoulder for a woman as stubborn as Jane to get the message.

"All right, I'll make time for coffee," he said, although he wasn't happy about it. He wanted her off his ranch and out of his life *now,* while he had the strength to let her leave.

He walked into the house, reheated the coffee and poured them each a mug. He carried the mugs out to the porch; no need to sit inside on an afternoon as pleasant as this.

"You didn't mention going into partnership with your uncle when you finished your assignment here," he said bluntly.

"No," she said. "It's always been accepted by the family that I would and—"

"It's all right, Jane, you don't need to explain it to me."

Her relief was obvious. "I should have said something much sooner, I know, but I didn't want you to get the wrong idea."

He stared into the distance, training his eyes on the rolling hills nestled against the horizon. It was either that or look at her, and he didn't think he could do that and still say what he had to say.

"You're a very good doctor," he began, and the compliment was sincere. "If I hadn't realized that earlier, you proved it the day we found Richard Weston."

"Thank you."

"You'll be a valuable asset to your uncle's practice."

"I'm not quite sure that's what…" She faltered, and he could see she was having a difficult time.

"Listen, Jane, I've been doing some thinking and I believe it'd be best if we suspended our lessons."

His words were met with stunned silence. "You're serious, aren't you?"

"Very."

"Just because I *might* be joining my uncle's medical practice? I haven't even made up my mind about that! I wish you'd hear me out first."

"No." This was important. "Because you belong in California."

"Hogwash."

"You might adapt to life here in Texas for a while, but it isn't going to last. The writing's on the wall."

"And just when did you become a handwriting expert?"

"Last night."

She snorted. "Oh, come on, Ca—"

Cal interrupted her. "I was wrong. You aren't Dr. Texas, you're Dr. Big City. Big plans. Big bucks, platinum charge cards, high-powered friends."

Jane vaulted to her feet, spilling her coffee on the porch. "Don't give me that, Phillip Calvin Patterson."

He was surprised she knew his full name, but this wasn't the time to ask how come she did.

"You know what the real problem is, don't you?" She dragged in a deep breath, preparing to answer her own question. "You're a coward."

"I'm not going to trade insults with you, if that's what you're looking for," he said.

"I'm not stupid."

"I didn't say you were."

Hands on her hips, she threw her head back and glared at the sky. "You might as well have said it," she returned, calmer now. "I love you and I'm fairly certain you feel the same way about me."

"You're taking a lot for granted."

"Perhaps, I am," she agreed, "but if you're idiotic enough to send me away because you're afraid..."

His eyes flared at the word.

"Afraid," she repeated, "then you're a fool, as well."

"It might be best if you left," he said. His head was beginning to pound again. He wasn't up to dealing with a tirade.

"If that's what you want, I will. And I won't be back—"

"That's what I was hoping," he said, and hated himself for being so cruel.

"—unless you ask," she finished as though he hadn't spoken.

With her head held high, she walked in the direction of her parked car, then stopped halfway across the yard. For a moment he figured she was planning to argue with him some more, but he was wrong. Instead, she turned toward the corral where Atta Girl stood, her sleek neck stretched over the top rail.

Jane stroked the mare's nose and whatever she said apparently met with Atta Girl's approval, because the animal nodded and snorted. Climbing onto the bottom fence rail, Jane put her arms around Atta Girl's neck and hugged her. Then she leaped down, stroked Atta Girl's nose again and walked over to her car and climbed inside.

A minute later she was gone. She'd retained her dignity—and his heart.

Chapter Ten

Jane had called Cal Patterson a coward and a fool, and she'd meant it. Add to that stubborn, unreasonable, infuriating...and worse.

Dr. Big City. Big plans. Big bucks. Each time his words came to mind she grew more furious. After all the time she'd spent with him how could he know so little about her? That really hurt.

By Thursday she was exhausted. Sleep eluded her and she'd rarely been so frustrated or out of sorts.

Ellie stopped by the clinic late Thursday afternoon when the office was technically closed. Jenny led her back to the office, where Jane sat making a desultory attempt to organize the top of her desk.

"I take it this is a personal visit," Jane said after Jenny had left.

"Have you got a few minutes?" Ellie asked.

Jane nodded. "For you I do, but not if you're here to talk about Cal."

"Fair enough," Ellie said, entering the room. She sat in the chair across from Jane's desk.

"You know what infuriates me most?" Jane blurted, her anger spilling over. "It's that Cal didn't have the common decency to talk this over with me. Oh no, he just *assumes* I'm returning to California without so much as waiting to hear my side."

"Jane, I thought you didn't want to talk about him."

"Forget I said that." Jane shook her head. "And you know? That's not the worst of it," she went on. "Not only doesn't he hear me out, he sends me away like I'm a child he can order around."

"I'll admit—"

Jane interrupted her. "He was completely out of line in what he said. If he didn't want to see me again, fine, but to insult me—that was going too far."

"He insulted you?" Ellie sounded appropriately outraged.

"Tell me, do I look like a big-city doctor to you?" Jane demanded without expecting a response. "I don't even wear makeup any more. Well, maybe a little mascara and lipstick, but that's all. I haven't washed my car in months. I wear jeans practically all the time." She took a deep breath. "And when's the last time you saw a big-city doctor asking some disgruntled rancher to teach her how to ride? A rancher who implies that this supposed big-city doctor is only interested in money, by the way."

"He said that?" Ellie was clearly shocked.

"Sort of. And more—like it was time I left."

"Cal suggested you leave Promise?"

"No, the ranch, which I did, but not before I put in my two cents' worth."

"Good for you!"

"I told him he was a coward."

Ellie's eyes widened. "You told Cal *what?*"

"That he's a coward, and I said it to his face."

"What did *he* say?"

Jane paused and tried to remember. "Nothing."

"Nothing?"

"Nothing memorable, anyway."

Ellie clapped her hands, apparently enjoying the details of Jane's final skirmish with Cal. Her outrage, however, only helped so much. "I hope you're here to tell me how utterly miserable he is." It would boost Jane's deflated ego to learn he was pining away for her.

"Actually," Ellie said, her gaze warm with sympathy, "I haven't seen him, so I can't. But Glen has."

"Oh?" Jane's spirits lifted hopefully.

"Apparently Cal's been pretty closemouthed about you."

Those same spirits sank again, even lower than before.

"But Glen did say Cal's been in a bitch of a mood."

Jane couldn't have held back a smile to save her soul. So...the man was suffering. Good.

"I don't mean to be nosy—" Ellie's gaze shifted uncomfortably to her hands "—but what happened? Everything seemed to be going so nicely."

"You tell me!" Jane cried. "My parents arrived as a birthday surprise, and we went to dinner and Cal joined us."

"So he's met your parents."

"Yes, but I rue the day. No," she said, changing

her mind, "I'm glad it happened before..." She hesitated. "Actually, it's too late for that."

"You're falling in love with Cal?" Ellie asked bluntly.

"I've already fallen." Might as well admit it. "I felt close to him—closer than I have to anyone. For the first time since my college days there was someone in my life who..." She let the rest fade.

Ellie was silent for a minute. "You weren't far off, you know."

"About what?"

"Cal being a coward. He *is* afraid."

"Of what? Me moving back to California? Give me a break, Ellie. I've been here less than a year and my contract's for three. Do I need to decide right this minute if I'm going to live in Promise for the rest of my life?"

"No."

Jane ignored the response, too keyed up to stop now. "He's being more than a little unreasonable, if you ask me."

"I agree with you."

"I'm not another Jennifer Healy."

"I know that. Glen knows that. You know that," Ellie said.

"But not Cal."

"Not Cal."

Jane brushed a stray hair from her face. "I told him I loved him," she said, revealing the most intimate and embarrassing part of their argument. She'd exposed her heart to him, and he'd not only dismissed *her* feelings, he'd denied his own.

"Oh, Jane, just be patient. He'll figure it out. Eventually."

"He might have offered me a reason to stay," she said, her voice little more than a whisper.

Ellie sighed expressively. "I don't know what it is about men in Texas. They're stubborn as the day is long."

"Proud, too," Jane added. "Way too proud."

"Impatient."

"Uncommunicative."

Ellie nodded, then sighed again. "Wonderful. Loving. Protective and gentle and passionate."

Jane closed her eyes, not wanting to confuse the issue with anything positive.

"Are you going to Caroline and Grady's wedding on Saturday?" Ellie asked her, abruptly changing the subject.

"Caroline asked me to cut the cake."

"Cal will be there," Ellie warned.

"Cal is Grady's best man." For half a heartbeat Jane toyed with the idea of finding an excuse to skip the wedding, but she refused to let Cal Patterson influence where she went or what she did. "I'd better get used to seeing him around town," Jane said, more for her own sake than Ellie's. "We won't be able to avoid running into each other now and then."

A saucy grin appeared on Ellie's face. "That's exactly what I was thinking. Cal's going to see you at the wedding. He'll see you at the grocery store and the Chili Pepper and bingo. And every time he goes to the post office he'll drive by the clinic."

"Heaven help him if he gets sick," Jane said.

"That would be horrible, wouldn't it?" Ellie said, sounding almost gleeful at the prospect.

"Absolutely horrible," Jane agreed.

Ellie shivered delightedly. "I can hardly wait."

Jane laughed for the first time in days. "I can't wait to give this stubborn Texas rancher a booster shot in places men don't like to talk about."

THE LAST NIGHT of the three-day midweek cruise, Dovie decided to join Mary and Phil Patterson in the lounge for drinks and dancing. Mary had been after her the entire trip to make herself more accessible to the single men on board, but Dovie couldn't see the point.

The music was from the forties and fifties, and judging by the crowd on the dance floor, the audience appreciated it.

"I'm so glad you decided to join us," Mary said, greeting Dovie at the door and leading her to a small table at the back of the room.

"I couldn't see spending our last night aboard doing something silly like sleeping," Dovie teased.

Mary patted her hand. "I wish you'd enjoyed the cruise more."

"But I did," Dovie assured her friend. It had been the perfect escape. Being away from Frank had given her some perspective on the relationship and on the difficulties she and Frank had encountered.

A waiter came for her drink order, and Dovie asked for a glass of white wine. Maybe what she needed was a little something to loosen her inhibitions. Actually she felt better than she had in weeks—although she still missed Frank.

"I couldn't believe the way you took to the water! I wouldn't have guessed you were that much of a swimmer."

It'd been years since she'd gone swimming, but Dovie'd had no intention of wasting an opportunity like this. For her, the highlight of the cruise had been snorkeling off the Yucatán Peninsula. Viewing the different species of colorful and exotic sea life was an experience she would long remember. She said as much to Mary.

"But your thoughts were on Frank," Mary replied.

Dovie couldn't deny it. Three days away, and she was dreadfully homesick, feeling more than a little lost and confused. Mostly she was angry with herself for having done something as foolish as putting her home up for sale. Promise was where she belonged, and she wasn't about to let Frank Hennessey chase her away. Dovie didn't blame Frank, but herself; she'd simply overreacted to his dating Tammy Lee.

The music started again and Phil stood, ready to escort his wife onto the dance floor.

Mary hesitated.

"Go on, you two," Dovie urged, her own foot tapping to the music.

To her surprise, no more than thirty seconds had passed before a distinguished-looking man approached her table. "Would you care to dance?"

Dovie stared at him as if this was the most complex question she'd ever been asked. "Yes," she said, deciding suddenly. She stood up and placed her hand in his.

"I'm Gordon Pawling," he said as he slid his arm around her waist and guided her onto the dance floor.

"Dovie Boyd," she said.

"I know."

She looked at him in surprise. "How?"

"I asked your friends the first night of the cruise."

Dovie remembered Mary mentioning a tall handsome man who'd questioned her about Dovie. While it had salved her ego to know that someone had asked to meet her, Dovie wasn't interested in a holiday romance. The only man she'd ever loved other than her husband was Frank Hennessey. She still did love Frank. She wasn't a woman who loved lightly or gave her heart easily.

The crowded floor forced Dovie and her partner to dance more closely than she would have liked. Gordon, too, seemed uncomfortable with the way they were shoved together, but as the dance went on, they both relaxed.

She liked him. He didn't talk her ear off with tales of how successful or well-known he was. He simply held her close. It surprised her how good it felt to be in a man's arms again, even if the man was little more than a stranger.

When the number was finished, Gordon escorted her back to the table. "Thank you, Dovie."

"Thank *you*."

Mary and Phil approached.

"He's a lucky man, whoever he is," Gordon said.

Dovie frowned, wondering how he knew she was

in love with someone else. Mary must have said something.

"I see you've met your admirer," Mary said, dabbing her handkerchief on her damp brow. "Won't you join us—Gordon, isn't it?"

Gordon looked to Dovie to second the invitation.

She could see no harm in it. "Please," she said, and gestured toward the empty chair next to her own.

"Thank you."

Gordon bought a round of drinks.

"Phil Patterson," Phil said, stretching his hand across the table for Gordon to shake.

"Gordon Pawling."

"Where are you from, Gordon?" Mary asked.

"Toronto, Canada."

Phil nodded. "I understand that's a beautiful city."

"It is," Gordon agreed.

"We're from Texas," Mary said, and Dovie nearly laughed out loud. No one listening to their accent would have guessed anywhere else.

"A little town in the hill country called Promise," Phil put in.

"Promise," Gordon repeated.

"Dovie owns an antique store there." Mary's voice held a note of pride.

"And we have the bed-and-breakfast," Phil added.

"I'm a retired judge," Gordon said.

"A judge." Mary's eyebrows rose slightly as she glanced at Dovie. She seemed to be saying that Gordon was a catch she shouldn't let slip through her fingers.

"Retired," Gordon was quick to remind them. "I haven't served on the bench for three years now."

"Do you travel much?" Mary asked. "Is that how you're spending your retirement?"

"Let's dance, Mary," her husband said pointedly. He got up and didn't give his wife much of an option.

Mary's reluctance showed as she rose to her feet.

As soon as they were out of earshot, Dovie felt she should apologize for Mary's questions. "You'll have to forgive my friend," Dovie said. "It's just that Mary's encouraging me to see other men." Once the words left her lips, she realized more explanation was required. "I've been seeing someone...in Promise...for quite a few years. We had a difference of opinion and now he's dating another woman." It hurt to say the words even to someone she wasn't likely to see after tonight.

Gordon reached across the table and squeezed her hand. "I need to revise my opinion of your male friend. He didn't know a treasure when he found it."

Dovie smiled. "Have you been talking to Mary?"

Gordon's smile was gentle. "No."

Dovie looked toward the dance floor and smiled, too. "Shall we?" she asked, preferring that they dance rather than discuss her relationship with Frank.

"It'd be my pleasure." Gordon stood and offered Dovie his hand.

They danced every dance for the rest of the night.

At midnight they attended the buffet. Dovie's appetite had been lacking; even the lavish display of pastries and other goodies hadn't tempted her. Not once during the three days had she stayed awake long enough to partake of the midnight buffet.

Tonight, however, she was famished. Gordon Pawling filled his plate, and Dovie wasn't shy about helping herself, either. Mary and Phil were right behind them in the buffet line.

"I'm going to have to diet for a month after this," Mary complained.

"Make that two," Phil teased, and Mary elbowed him in the ribs.

Too full to think about sleeping, Dovie gladly accepted Gordon's invitation for a stroll on the deck when they'd finished eating.

The night was beautiful. Out in the middle of the Gulf of Mexico, miles from land and the lights of the city, the stars blazed, filling the sky.

"I don't think I've ever seen so many stars," Dovie said, leaning against the ship's railing.

"In Northern Ontario," Gordon said, "in the dead of winter when it seems like spring is only a distant promise, the stars look like this. When a fresh snowfall reflects the moonlight and starlight, it's almost as bright as day."

"It sounds lovely," Dovie said wistfully. "I've never been to Canada," she confessed. "I'm afraid I'm not much of a traveler. This is my first cruise."

"Mine, too."

"I wouldn't have come if it wasn't for Mary and Phil. Mary thought it was what I needed—to get away for a time."

"Was it?"

"Yes," she admitted after a moment. "I think it was exactly the right thing to do."

"I came because of my son."

Dovie heard the smile in his voice.

"Bill seemed to think that two years was enough time for me to grieve the loss of his mother. He insisted I take a cruise, and when I balked, he purchased the ticket himself and presented it to me on my birthday."

"He sounds like a determined young man."

"Very much so," Gordon said. "He's a younger version of me, I fear. He followed in my footsteps and seems headed for the bench."

"Your wife's been gone two years, then?"

"Yes," he said, and sadness weighted his words. "I loved her for forty years and I don't know if it's possible for me to love anyone else."

"It is possible," Dovie told him. Her own experience had taught her that.

"I'm beginning to think you're right," he said.

They turned away from the railing and Gordon tucked her hand in the crook of his arm. They walked together in silence, their pace leisurely, and they spoke of their lives and marriages and dreams.

An hour later she still wasn't tired, but they'd be disembarking the next morning and things would be hectic. She knew she should get some sleep.

Gordon escorted Dovie to her cabin. "Thank you," she murmured. The night had been perfect in every way.

"All the appreciation is mine," Gordon said, then

very slowly leaned forward and kissed her on the lips.

Dovie blinked back sudden tears.

Gordon reached into his suit jacket and pulled out a business card. "My home phone number is listed here," he said. "In case things don't work out with your friend…"

Dovie accepted the card.

"Will you call?" he asked.

"I…I don't know." She didn't want to lead him into believing something might come of this one night.

"I'm very grateful to you, Dovie Boyd," he said. "For this evening. And for showing me that my son might possibly be right."

But Dovie was the one who needed to thank him. She'd learned something, too.

Her life could go on without Frank. And in time, she might fall in love again.…

CAL WAS AWARE of Jane's presence the minute he escorted Savannah Smith down the church aisle. Grady's sister was serving as matron of honor to Caroline Daniels, and he was best man.

Every pew in Promise Christian Church was filled. It seemed as if half the town—and half the county—had come to Caroline and Grady's wedding. Being the postmistress, Caroline knew just about everyone, and they knew and liked her. Grady, too. The integrity with which he'd handled Richard's debts was no small thing, and the merchants of Promise felt both gratitude and respect. This was a chance for the townspeople and ranchers to show

how much Grady and Caroline meant to their community.

Cal didn't see Jane, but he knew she was in the church. He *felt* her there, and as hard as he tried to ignore her, he found it impossible. After walking with Savannah down the aisle, Cal joined Grady, who stood next to the altar. The organ music swelled through the sanctuary as Caroline appeared at the back of the church.

Cal heard Grady's soft intake of breath as he gazed at his bride. Caroline looked lovely in her dress, complete with veil and a long train. Cal smiled as he glanced at Maggie, wearing a green velvet dress for her role as flower girl.

Then his eyes sought out Jane. She sat on the bride's side, wearing a pearl white suit with big gold buttons. Accustomed to seeing her in jeans and a Western shirt, he didn't recognize her for a moment. Damn, but she was beautiful.

Cal forced his attention away from her and looked at Caroline, whom Frank Hennessey was walking down the aisle. He soon found his gaze wandering back to Jane. Her eyes refused to meet his, which was just as well.

He regretted the way they'd parted. Both of them had been angry, saying hurtful things, things they didn't mean. He'd told himself that sometimes it was necessary to be cruel to be kind—only in this case he was the one who'd suffered. He'd been miserable and lonely since that day. He knew their confrontation hadn't been easy for her, either, but she certainly seemed to be faring better than he was.

She might still be angry, but after a while she'd

see that this was for the best. When the time came, she'd return to the life she'd always known in California. Her career plans were already in place—and they didn't include practicing medicine in rural America. They didn't include falling in love with a rancher.

The organ music faded, and Caroline joined Grady at the front of the church. Wade McMillen stepped forward to preside over the ceremony, smiling at the happy couple.

Before Caroline and Grady exchanged their vows, Wade had a few words to say about love and marriage.

Since he intended never to fall in love again, Cal only listened with half an ear. It wasn't until Wade said, "Love doesn't come with any guarantees," that Cal paid attention.

That was what he'd wanted. A guarantee. He wanted Jane to promise she'd never leave him. He'd been waiting for her to assure him that her future would always include him.

Without that guarantee, he hadn't been willing to take the risk.

The remainder of the ceremony was a blur in Cal's mind. He handed Grady the wedding band at the appropriate moment and escorted Savannah back down the center aisle following the ceremony.

Later, at the reception, he stood in the receiving line and exchanged chitchat with the guests as they paused to greet the newlyweds and other members of the wedding party.

Grady and Caroline were ecstatic. Maggie was with them and proudly referred to Grady as her daddy. As Cal watched he felt a sharp emptiness in the pit of his stomach. Overnight Grady had a wife and a daughter, and he'd pledged his life to them with nothing to safeguard the future. He'd stood before his family, friends and God and promised to love Caroline for the rest of his life. Without knowing what the next day held, or the next year. Whatever the future might bring, he was willing to love Caroline and Maggie.

The emptiness inside Cal increased. He loved Jane, but unless he was offered a money-back guarantee, he hadn't been willing to risk his heart by telling her how he felt.

When he lost Jennifer, he'd simply stepped aside and let her walk out of his life without saying one word to stop her. He'd done the same thing with Jane, only this time he'd loved much more deeply. Because of that, he hadn't just let her go; he'd pushed her out the door with both hands.

He'd refused to commit himself to the love he felt. Not without reassurances first.

As the wedding guests progressed down the receiving line, Cal saw Jane moving toward him. His heart reacted immediately, leaping with a rush of excitement at the mere sight of her. His mind buzzed with ideas of what he should say. Something pithy, something profound; he couldn't decide what.

Before he had the opportunity to display his wit and charm, she was there, standing in front of him, her hand in his.

"Hello, Cal," she said. Her eyes seemed to sear right through him. Then without warning she proceeded to the next person in line.

Cal yearned to call her back, to say he deserved more than a casual greeting, but he couldn't. The next guests stood directly in front of him and he was obliged to greet them.

Cal continued to greet the wedding guests. Whenever he could, he sought out Jane with his eyes. He saw her serve wedding cake and chat with each person, joking and laughing. If she was miserable without him, he'd be hard pressed to prove it.

He recalled the first few months after Jane had moved to Promise and how the people in town had avoided her. The fault had been on both sides. Jane had arrived with her newfangled ideas and big-city attitude, and folks in town hadn't been too tolerant. There'd been some unwarranted assumptions made by Jane, but also by the people of Promise.

All that had changed in the past two months. Jane had mellowed, made new friends, gained the confidence of people here. He remembered the night Jeremy Bishop had broken his arm and the gentleness she'd displayed to both the boy and his terrified mother.

Little Maggie Daniels had brought her the rag doll because she knew Dr. Jane could be trusted.

Cal had seen for himself her passion for medicine and the way she'd squared off against death, fighting every way she knew how to save Richard Weston's life.

Damn it all, he was in love with her, and his feelings weren't likely to change. If he wanted a guarantee for the future, he wasn't going to find one. Not with Jane. Not with any woman.

He hadn't liked it when Jane called him a coward. Even now it wasn't easy to admit she'd been right.

The cake was almost gone before Cal found the courage to approach the table.

"Is there a piece for me?" he asked.

Jane glanced up and he could tell by the look on her face that she was surprised to see him.

"I believe there are a few pieces left," she said cordially enough, but she gave herself away when she refused to meet his eyes. She reached for a plate and handed it to him.

He cleared his throat and said, "You look very pretty."

"Thank you. I bought this suit in downtown Los Angeles."

Cal let the comment slide. "Something's wrong with Atta Girl." He said the first thing that came to mind.

That got her attention. "What?"

"It's nothing to worry about," he told her, then grabbed a glass of punch and walked away. That was a dirty trick, but he was willing to use whatever he had to.

Cal found a vacant table at the other end of the hall and sat down. He hadn't been there a minute when Jane pulled out a chair and joined him.

"What's wrong with Atta Girl?" she demanded.

"She misses you," Cal said between bites of cake.

Jane stared at him as if she hadn't understood a word.

"I miss you, too," he said, swallowing his pride along with the wedding cake.

"Oh, Cal."

"Do they have cattle ranches in California?" he asked.

Her brow puckered in a frown. "I don't know—I'm sure they must."

"Good. I was thinking of moving there."

"To California?" Her voice rose a full octave. "In the name of heaven, *why?*"

This was where it became difficult, but having made his decision, he wasn't going to renege now. "Looks like I'm going to have to if I want to be near you."

Jane was on her feet so fast the chair nearly toppled backward. "You're taking a lot for granted, Cal Patterson."

"Perhaps," he agreed, recognizing his own response the day they'd argued and she told him he loved her. "But the way I figure it, if we're going to get married and you've already agreed to join your uncle's medical practice, this is the only solution."

Jane glared at him as though it was all she could do not to slap him.

"You *are* going to marry me, aren't you?" he asked.

Chapter Eleven

Back less than twenty-four hours from her cruise, Dovie worked endlessly in the church kitchen, helping the women's group with Caroline and Grady's wedding. She had artfully arranged hors d'oeuvres on silver platters and set them on the counter to be picked up.

Actually Dovie was grateful to be in here, away from the reception, although it was considered the least enviable of the jobs the women's group performed for weddings and other social events. At least while she was here, she needn't fear seeing Frank dance with Tammy Lee or flirt with any other women.

She hadn't seen him since her return, but then, it was still early. She steeled herself for their next confrontation, dreading it already.

Humming softly to herself, Edwina Moorhouse entered the kitchen. "Pastor McMillen is looking for you."

"Me?" Dovie couldn't imagine what he wanted.

"He asked me to send you to his office."

"Really?" Dovie washed her hands and reached for a towel. "Did he happen to mention what this was about?"

"Not a word," the older woman said.

But Dovie noticed that Edwina's eyes were twinkling. If she didn't know better, she'd think Wade and the Moorhouse sisters had something up their sleeves.

Tucking a stray curl behind her ear, Dovie left the kitchen. Pastor McMillen's office was just down the hallway and around the corner. His door was closed and she tapped on it politely.

"Come in," he called.

Dovie opened the door, and the first person she saw was Frank Hennessey, rising to his feet from a chair opposite Wade's desk. The sheriff also stood when she entered the room, his eyes focused intently on her. Dovie's pulse accelerated to an alarming rate, and she was grateful when Wade motioned for her to take a seat.

"Hello, Dovie," Frank said.

"Frank." She nodded once, but avoided looking in his direction. He sat down when she did.

"Actually I need to get back to the wedding," Wade announced. "My purpose here is to bring the two of you together to talk this out." With that, he left the room.

Dovie was too shocked to speak.

"I asked Wade to bring you here," Frank explained.

"Why?"

"Well, because I didn't think you'd come if I asked."

"I mean, why did you want to talk to me? As far as I can see, everything's already been said. You're dating other women now."

"One date, Dovie, and that was a disaster." He got to his feet and walked across the room to stare out the window. "There's only one woman I love and that's you."

"That's all well and good, but it hasn't gotten us very far to this point, has it?"

"No," he agreed with a certain reluctance.

Dovie's mind whirled. She couldn't imagine that Wade McMillen, a man of God, would condone Frank and her resuming their previous relationship, especially considering its physical aspects.

"You talked to Wade about us?" she asked.

"Actually he came to me."

"Wade?" Dovie had never heard of such a thing.

"I've been feeling pretty down lately," Frank admitted. "I assumed that once you saw me with Tammy Lee, you'd realize how much you missed me and want me back."

Dovie's mouth thinned with irritation.

"I don't think any idea of mine has backfired worse. I accept the blame for that—it was a sign of how desperate I was without you."

It didn't hurt Dovie's feelings any to learn he'd had a miserable time with Tammy Lee.

"Then you left on the cruise and...and I worried the entire time that you'd meet someone else." He hesitated, then asked, "Did you...meet someone?"

"Yes, a retired judge. He lives in Toronto."

"Oh." Frank turned to face her, eyes narrowed. "Will you be seeing him again?"

"I...I..."

"Don't answer that," Frank said, holding up his hand. "It's none of my business. Like I started to say, while you were away, I was pretty miserable. But then, nothing's been right since we split. Wade and I had a long talk, and I told him about you and me."

Dovie could feel the color fill her face even before she asked the question. "You didn't mention anything about...spending the night at my house, did you?"

"Yes."

"Oh, Frank, how could you?" She covered her face with both hands.

"He isn't going to judge us, Dovie," Frank hastened to assure her. "It's not his job. He told me that himself."

It was one thing for Frank to refuse to marry her, but to embarrass her in front of the pastor was something else entirely.

"I explained to Wade why I've had such a struggle with this marriage idea."

She hoped he'd done a better job of it with Wade than he had with her. As far as she was concerned, telling her he wasn't "the marrying kind" was a mighty poor excuse!

"I've lived alone all these years, and a man grows

accustomed to having things his own way—to certain freedoms." He paused and his eyes pleaded with hers for understanding. "These freedoms I'm talking about don't have anything to do with other women, either."

"We've been through all this before," Dovie said, tired of the same old argument. She didn't want to hear his excuses again, especially when she could practically recite them herself.

"I couldn't find any solution to it, either," Frank said, his voice gaining speed and volume. "But, Dovie, don't you see, that's been the whole problem."

"What do you mean?"

"Wade said we'd overlooked the obvious solution, and by God, he's right. We can get married and I can still have my freedom."

"How?" she asked incredulously.

Frank's smile lit up his entire face. "It's so obvious I can't believe we didn't see it earlier. I'll keep my house and you keep yours. Some nights I'll spend with you—and if you want, you can sleep over at my house, too."

Dovie's head came up.

"I won't feel the walls closing in on me, but at the same time you'd have what you want. You'd be my wife, Dovie."

If she was tongue-tied earlier, it didn't compare to what she was now.

Frank's eyes were bright with hope as he reached for her hands. "Dovie Boyd, would you do me the honor of becoming my bride?"

She blinked back tears and smiled so hard it hurt. "Oh, Frank, I love you so much. Yes, I'll marry you." It was all she'd ever wanted. It didn't matter what other people thought or said. This was a plan that worked for *them*.

She didn't know who moved first, but they were in each other's arms and kissing.

God bless Wade McMillen, Dovie mused as Frank's lips found hers.

IF CAL PATTERSON made her cry now, with half the town looking on, Jane swore she'd never forgive him.

He held her gaze, his feelings for her glowing in his eyes. "I'm asking you to be my wife."

She brought her hand to her forehead. "I heard you the first time." Which, she had to admit in retrospect, wasn't a very gracious thing to say.

"Do you want me to get down on one knee in front of all these people, Jane?" he asked. Cal was standing now, too.

"No." She shook her head and retreated a step.

"I've got an engagement ring. It's a good one, big diamond and only slightly used, but I'm afraid the damn thing's cursed. If you don't mind, I'd prefer to buy you a new one. I'm hoping Harley will take the other as a trade-in."

"You'd sell your share of the ranch?" she asked, afraid she'd been hearing things.

"If I had to."

"Why?" she demanded.

"Because I love you."

Damn, he'd done it to her. Jane could feel the tears welling in her eyes, threatening to spill down her cheeks.

"After what Wade said earlier, I've given up demanding guarantees. Like the preacher said, love just doesn't come with one. I don't know what the future holds for either of us. All I know about my future is that I want you in it."

Jane pressed her index fingers under her eyes in a desperate effort to keep the tears at bay. "You make me weep in public, Cal Patterson, and I swear you'll live to regret it."

"You'd cry for me?"

"Yes, you fool!"

His lazy grin spread from ear to ear. "That's the most beautiful thing you've ever said to me."

"Oh, puh-leeze!" She whirled around while she could still see straight and stormed across the room. She wasn't surprised to find that Cal had followed her.

The music started, and after Caroline and Grady had danced the first number, other couples stepped onto the floor.

"I'm not light on my feet, but I'd be willing to give it a try, if you are," Cal said, offering her his hand.

Jane didn't think she could refuse him anything at that moment. She placed her hand in his and nearly sighed aloud when he touched her. The sense of rightness she felt in his arms was...miraculous. Incredible. And so exciting.

Cal's chin rubbed the side of her face. "You love me, don't you?" he whispered.

"You know I do."

"I love you, too, Dr. Texas."

"You're serious about moving to California?"

"If that's what it takes to be close to you."

It astonished her that he'd agree to leave Promise. It shocked her, moved her deeply, inspired her. "As it happens, I love living here," she whispered, resting her head on his shoulder. She closed her eyes and savored the feel of his arms around her.

"You'd be willing to live here?" he asked.

"Promise needs a doctor, doesn't it? Everyone here feels like family. I enjoy the challenge of my job. It didn't take me long to realize that joining Uncle Ken wasn't really what I wanted." She shook her head. "Before I came to Promise, I just didn't have enough experience to know that."

"What about your uncle?"

"He'll be disappointed, but he'll get over it."

"Your parents?"

"Give them time and they'll learn to love Willie Nelson as much as they do the Beach Boys."

"And me?"

"That may take some doing," she teased. "However, if you promise to make them grandparents…"

His arms tightened about her waist. "I'm feeling this very strong urge to kiss you, and either I embarrass us both right here and now or we sneak outside.''

Jane smiled softly, so much in love that the emotion burned inside her. "I don't know about you, but I could do with a bit of fresh air."

In the middle of the song Cal stopped dancing, clasped her hand and led her off the dance floor.

Ellie Patterson lifted her head from Glen's shoulder, looking worried. Jane smiled broadly and gave her a thumbs-up. Ellie signaled back with a wink and laid her head back on her husband's shoulder again.

Once they were outside in the shadows of the church, Cal pulled Jane into his arms. She went there without resistance. His mouth found hers and his tongue licked the edges of her lips. With a small sigh of welcome, she opened her heart and her life to him. They kissed with a need that was so deep she forgot to breathe.

"You'll marry me?" he asked, his voice a whisper.

"Yes." The decision had already been made for her the instant he asked. She'd known then that this was what she wanted, that Promise was where she belonged. This was her home now, with Cal.

"When?"

"You in a hurry?" she asked, grinning delightedly. She couldn't see any reason to wait, either, not when they both knew what they wanted. Even waiting another minute seemed too long.

"You're damn straight I'm in a hurry," Cal said. "Let's talk to Wade right now."

Jane laughed and hugged him close. "Just remember, the future has no guarantees, Rebel."

"Well, it does come with at least one," he said, lifting her several inches off the ground. "My love for you."

"And mine for you," she whispered before her lips met his.

* * * * *

Next month, join your friends in Promise
for the annual rodeo and chili cookoff!
Then sit back and watch some of the changes
that are going to take place...
A stranger comes into Nell Bishop's life.
Savannah's baby is born.
And the secret history of Bitter End
is finally revealed.
Look for NELL'S COWBOY in June.

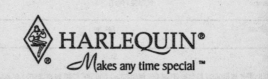

Take 4 bestselling love stories FREE

Plus get a FREE surprise gift!

Special Limited-time Offer

Mail to Harlequin Reader Service®

3010 Walden Avenue
P.O. Box 1867
Buffalo, N.Y. 14240-1867

YES! Please send me 4 free Harlequin Romance® novels and my free surprise gift. Then send me 6 brand-new novels every month, which I will receive months before they appear in bookstores. Bill me at the low price of $2.90 each plus 25¢ delivery and applicable sales tax if any*. That's the complete price and a savings of over 10% off the cover prices—quite a bargain! I understand that accepting the books and gift places me under no obligation ever to buy any books. I can always return a shipment and cancel at any time. Even if I never buy another book from Harlequin, the 4 free books and the surprise gift are mine to keep forever.

116 HEN CE63

Name	(PLEASE PRINT)
Address	Apt. No.
City	State	Zip

This offer is limited to one order per household and not valid to present Harlequin Romance® subscribers. *Terms and prices are subject to change without notice. Sales tax applicable in N.Y.

UROM-696   ©1990 Harlequin Enterprises Limited

DEBBIE MACOMBER's
MIDNIGHT SONS

Don't miss the six books in this wonderful miniseries!

Midnight Sons Miniseries

#03379	Brides for Brothers	$2.99 U.S.☐	$3.50 CAN.☐
#03383	The Marriage Risk	$2.99 U.S.☐	$3.50 CAN.☐
#03387	Daddy's Little Helper	$2.99 U.S.☐	$3.50 CAN.☐
#03395	Because of the Baby	$3.25 U.S.☐	$3.75 CAN.☐
#03399	Falling For Him	$3.25 U.S.☐	$3.75 CAN.☐
#03403	Ending in Marriage	$3.25 U.S.☐	$3.75 CAN.☐

(quantities may be limited on some titles)

TOTAL AMOUNT $ _____
POSTAGE & HANDLING $ _____
($1.00 for one book, 50¢ for each additional)
APPLICABLE TAXES* $ _____
TOTAL PAYABLE $ _____
(check or money order—please do not send cash)

To order, complete this form and send it, along with a check or money order for the total above, payable to Harlequin Books, to: **In the U.S.:** 3010 Walden Avenue, P.O. Box 9047, Buffalo, NY 14269-9047; **In Canada:** P.O. Box 613, Fort Erie, Ontario, L2A 5X3.

Name: _____

Address: _____ City: _____

State/Prov.: _____ Zip/Postal Code: _____

*New York residents remit applicable sales taxes.
Canadian residents remit applicable GST and provincial taxes.

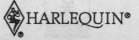

HARLEQUIN®

Look us up on-line at: http://www.romance.net   PHDMBACK

Welcome to *Love Inspired*™

A brand-new series of contemporary inspirational love stories.

Join men and women as they learn valuable lessons about facing the challenges of today's world and about life, love and faith.

Look for the following May 1998 Love Inspired™ titles:

A FAMILY TO CALL HER OWN by Irene Hannon

LOGAN'S CHILD by Lenora Worth

THERE COMES A SEASON by Carol Steward

Available in retail outlets in April 1998.

LIFT YOUR SPIRITS AND GLADDEN YOUR HEART

with *Love Inspired!*™

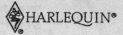

Not The Same Old Story!

 Exciting, glamorous romance stories that take readers around the world.

 Sparkling, fresh and tender love stories that bring you pure romance.

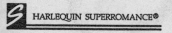 Bold and adventurous— Temptation is strong women, bad boys, great sex!

 Provocative and realistic stories that celebrate life and love.

 Contemporary fairy tales—where anything is possible and where dreams come true.

Heart-stopping, suspenseful adventures that combine the best of romance and mystery.

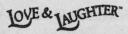 Humorous and romantic stories that capture the lighter side of love.